The Queen's Guide to Teapots and Pastries

Emma Steinbrecher

To my husband

Thank you for being the Cyris to my Isla. Thank you for sticking by me when I didn't have enough magic to keep teaching and decided to write books instead.

CONTENTS

Pronunciation Guide

Just in case you need it, here is a pronunciation guide for some of the words in this novella.

CHARACTERS

Cyris: sigh – russ

Isla: eye – luh

PLACES

Fairvein: fair – vein

Edessa: ed – ess – uh

ONE

I stared at the teapot for a solid hour. At least, that's what it felt like.

The morning had been slow, with hardly any customers, and I stood behind the counter in Isla's Teas and Treats, desperately trying to decode Clementine's strange gift. I'm sure it was a sight, my long brown hair piled atop my head, stray strands floating in all directions, my brows furrowed. It was, I'm certain, one of the most frustrating puzzles I had ever taken on.

Clementine was acquainted with objects and oddities, magical items that could do a number of wonders. Her shop up the way, Clementine's Parlor of the Extraordinary and Curious, kind of a long name if you ask me, was filled to the brim with strange trinkets.

This teapot had to do something.

It had to be special.

My eyes flicked up as the bell rang against the door, and I instantly straightened. The tourist season hadn't yet started in Fairvein, so I was certain that anyone coming into the shop was someone I knew. The island wasn't that big, and gossip traveled quickly. Any newcomers outside of the summer season would be talked about in great detail upon their arrival. There were no secrets here.

"Mrs. Elwood!" I walked around the counter, dodging the dried herbs hanging from the ceiling to greet her.

Mrs. Elwood smiled, the lines around her eyes becoming more prominent with the expression. "Dearest Isla," she began. "How is my favorite healer turned tea shop expert?"

"To be honest, Mrs. Elwood, a bit frustrated. Clementine gifted me that teapot, you know. I got it out about an hour ago and have been trying to figure out what it does exactly." I tucked a strand of hair behind my ear–rounded and plain, unlike the ears of the elven woman in front of me. "If I were telling the whole truth," I lowered my voice to a whisper, green eyes shining, no doubt. "The whole thing is a bit frightening. I'm afraid if I take off the lid, it may explode."

Mrs. Elwood let out a deep chuckle, one pulled from the pit of her belly. "I wouldn't be surprised."

"So," I started, "what can I do you for?" I glanced down, noticing a long strand of hair sticking to the white apron–brown. One of my own, then. I quickly and furiously brushed it away, sending it to the hardwood as I straightened the white linen laid over my simple sage dress.

When I looked up, Mrs. Elwood's expression had tightened. "Declan seems to think I'm a fool." I fought the urge to chuckle at her mention of her grandson. Declan, at the ripe age of fourteen, gave Mrs. Elwood a run for her money. His mother, Mrs. Elwood's daughter, had died during childbirth, and the elven woman had taken care of Declan ever since. "He went somewhere last night. I just know it, but he won't tell me where he'd gone. Do you have a tea that could help?"

I brushed the hair back from my face, turning to the wooden shelves lining the shop, rounding the tables and chairs set out for guests. The dried herbs weren't labeled particularly well, and organization was never my strength, but I could find what I needed easily enough.

"Laiaberry leaf tea," I supplied, grabbing a jar from the top shelf and moving it to the counter. I began weighing the herbs for a small bag. "It won't force him to tell the truth." My smile widened. "It will, however, inspire him to be a bit more honest."

Mrs. Elwood returned my smile, dropping a few coins in my hand before taking her tea. "You're the gem of Fairvein, Miss Isla," she said, and I fiddled with the hem of my apron.

"You're too kind," I responded.

"Have you heard of Queen Cranefield's travel brochure?" she asked.

Excitement immediately took over. "How could I not!" I said. "It's every shop owner's dream to be featured. I just wish she'd take a look at Fairvein. I'm surprised she hasn't, being a popular tourist site and all."

"That's just the thing." Mrs. Elwood leaned in, tucking a curly strand of silver hair behind her pointed ear. She still dwarfed me as she leaned across the counter, careful not to touch my strange teapot. "I heard whispers in town that she plans to scope out our shops here on the island. You could be featured."

"You can't be serious." I burst around the counter, squeezing the woman just short of stealing the breath from her lungs. Placing my hands on her shoulder, I reeled back, searching her eyes for the truth.

If Isla's Teas and Treats were featured in the Queen's travel brochure, business would pick up immediately. It would be the greatest gift I could think of.

"Quite serious," she said, peeling my hands from her shoulders. "I'm certain you'll be featured. Just watch for any newcomers to the shop. I heard she sends the very best to scope out the local stores prior to visiting herself. And since Fairvein is so small, I'm certain you'll be able to tell if someone new comes in." I smiled, hoping she was right. "I'm off to the bakery across the way. Cyris promised me one of those pastries with the jam in the center."

My smile fell. "Mrs. Elwood, you're welcome to any of the pastries in the glass cases."

Her smile was warm, despite the insult that followed. "Yes, dear. I know. Cyris is new, just starting though. And to be honest, he's quite talented."

I heard the underlying insult. So, my baking wasn't the best. It was perfectly suited for what I needed. I folded my arms across my chest, trying to hide my frustration. It was no use, but Mrs. Elwood didn't acknowledge it anyway.

"Oh, look!" she said. "Here he comes now."

A determined man shoved the glass door to my shop open, his brow creased as he muttered something under his breath. He stood with the door open, finally looking up to meet my gaze. Brown eyes, wireframed glasses, and a trimmed beard. Cyris was shorter than I imagined. I had only seen him from a distance at his bakery across the street. The shop was a new edition to the island, and of course, I'd been curious. Cyris hadn't grown up in Fairvein, so his arrival was part of the town's gossip.

"I've lost something," he said.

"I'm not sure how I can help," I responded, watching as he continued to hold the door open. "I'd appreciate it if you closed the door, though."

Just then, a harsh breeze whipped through the teashop, rattling the jars as the dried herbs hanging from the ceiling swayed.

"Ah," Cyris said. "There she is."

An air sprite spiraled through the shop, knocking over my jars and tilting my chairs like a tornado taking over the entire room.

I shrieked, desperately trying to catch everything before it came tumbling down. Mrs. Elwood screamed; Cyris laughed.

Giving up on the far wall, I scrambled to the counter as the air sprite zipped around my feet, sending me tumbling forward, slamming into the counter so hard the teapot tipped, tipped, and came crashing down on the floor.

I turned to give my best glare to the baker still laughing by the door as the air sprite returned to his vest pocket.

When I moved forward, my foot caught on a knocked-over chair, and I found myself on the hardwood, face down, embarrassed–*angry*.

I huffed as I shoved myself upward. Cyris was kneeling down before me and pushing up the white sleeves of the button-down beneath his vest. "My apologies," he said, sliding the glasses further up his nose. He was still smiling, and that only served to make me angrier. He extended a hand forward in an attempt to help me up.

My eyes flicked around the shop. There was *so much* to clean up. I would have to shut down for an entire day to fix it!

"I'm Cyris," he offered, that infuriating smile still plastered to his face. He smelled of plums and cinnamon. I immediately determined that it was a stupid scent.

I growled, pushing myself to stand and straightening my hair. Mrs. Elwood slipped out behind him as I fixed my dress, stomping my boot one time on the floor like a child. "And I'm *furious*," I seethed. "Get out!"

I pointed to the door, anger still bubbling in my chest as I watched Cyris exit the shop, turning back once before he left. The amused light in his eyes had me shrieking once more, fisting my hands at my sides before I turned to see my broken teapot.

No.

A perfectly intact teapot.

I could have sworn–

I deflated, leaning against the counter and touching the bruise I'm sure was forming on my cheek from the faceplant.

What an idiot, I thought, checking over the state of the shop one more time.

If only Clementine had gifted me an entire shop of jars that repaired themselves.

Instead, I was stuck with one gigantic mess, and for the first time in my life, as my eyes glanced through the glass door to see Cyris talking to Mrs. Elwood just outside of the bakery, I was also stuck with a heavy dose of hatred in my heart.

Two

I dragged the giant bag out of the tea shop, straining as I pushed the glass door open with my behind. Night had descended over Fairvein, and my blood had cooled significantly after my interaction with the ridiculous baker across the street, though the calm didn't last. Not when the door opened, and I placed the trash firmly against the front of my building, smelling the scent of baking bread wafting from across the street.

I kicked the bag once for good measure. Hopefully, the trash goblins, the ones that came in the night to collect the refuse, wouldn't mind if my garbage was a little beaten up.

The bag promptly tipped over, and I knelt to gather the spilled contents and tie the top even tighter.

I had to close the shop down for the rest of the day, spending my time sweeping and reorganizing–the latter being my least favorite activity.

Now, with sore muscles and a bruised ego, one that resulted from my face's very ungraceful acquaintance with the hardwood floor, I was ready to call it a night.

Maybe, I'd have better luck tomorrow.

"Would you like some help there?"

I finished repositioning the bag, my heart soaring at the offer. I had a second bag just inside the door.

"Would I?" I said brightly, spinning around to get a look at my savior. "That would be–"

My face fell. Cyris stood before me in the same emerald vest and white button-up shirt. His glasses reflected the fire from the street-lamps. "Oh," I said, rolling my eyes. "It's you."

I folded my arms across my chest, tapping my boot on the cobble-stone, awaiting an apology I was sure he'd come to deliver. Any decent elf, human, or otherwise would have.

"It's me," he responded before lifting a hand to gesture to me. "And it's you. Furious." A smile split his face, and I felt the rage bubble up all over again. I didn't like being angry–or maybe I did. Maybe I just liked being angry at *him*. "I never did inquire about the name," he continued. "Could you tell me how that happened? Were your parents–"

I grunted, stomping my foot once and clenching my fists at my side. "Stop talking," I groaned.

Cyris's smokey laugh bounced off the stones in the street, echoing loudly in my mind. "Of course."

"I don't want your help," I said, turning to kick the trash bag one more time. It was extremely satisfying, and now that the top was tightly secured, I didn't have to worry about the contents dumping again.

"It is late, though," he began, and I closed my eyes in frustration. I thought he had agreed to stop talking. "I could walk you home."

I faced him fully, folding my arms back over my chest so he could see how much his presence irked me. It did. Irk me, that is. "Unnecessary," I supplied, glancing at the pocket of his vest.

His brown eyes tracked the movement. "No sprites with me," he chuckled. "I can assure you of that."

I glared at him, harder than the agmund stones mined from the mountains of Edessa, the country Fairvein was a part of. "I wasn't–"

"Weren't you?" he interrupted. "Now, Furious. I'm sure you know full well." His smile widened. If that was even possible. "You wear your emotions quite plainly on that beautiful face of yours."

"Oh gross," I muttered, turning around to disappear into the store. Who in their right mind would first, destroy someone's shop in no more than one minute, and second, proceed to flirt with them that same evening in the street? *A crazy person*, I thought.

"Are you hoping to get a feature in the Queen's travel brochure?"

His question had me halting, luring me in like a siren that lived in the water around the island of Fairvein.

I looked back, refusing to turn around. "Possibly," I answered.

"Ah," he began, "I heard the tea shops, cafes, and bakeries were all placed under the same category." I turned around, noting the way his brown eyes still lit with amusement. Who in their right mind found life *this* amusing?

As I thought before, *a crazy person*.

"Okay?" I dragged the word out slowly, hoping it would push him to get to the point.

"That makes you, my dear Furious, direct competition."

I huffed. "Would you stop calling me that?" I straightened as his words sank in, marinating in my mind. "Wait," I said, narrowing my gaze.

Cyris cocked an eyebrow. "Yes?" He was enjoying this conversation far too much.

"Are you–" I glanced once at the trash still leaning against my building, proof of what had happened after he released a sprite in my store. My eyes flicked to him again, his form backed by the pale walls of the half-timbered bakery. "Are you threatening me?" I finished, though I wasn't sure he'd admit it.

"Why would I ever do that?" he asked, his expression too jovial for my liking.

I stepped forward, the shock written across my features. My eyebrows raised, and I pointed a finger at him, digging it into his firm chest. "Is that why you released a sprite into my shop?" I asked.

The whole plot was quite genius. He ruins my shop just in time for the Queen to send scouts to our city. It would make his bakery look better–secure him a place in the brochure if what Mrs. Elwood said about Cyris's jam pastries could be trusted.

I kept my gaze steady, leaning in so he could note how very serious I was. What a dirty, rotten player. It would be just like someone as infuriating as Cyris the baker to concoct such a nefarious plan.

His face fell, his brows pinching together. "Absolutely not," he said. "That was an honest mistake."

My eyes flicked between his, sizing him up. "I don't believe you."

His lip curled upward at one corner, and the crooked smile would have been quite handsome if he weren't such a poor sport. "Pity," he whispered before leaning in just slightly. He was too close, so I reeled back in disgust. That crooked grin couldn't work on me. Not ever. "I am quite the honorable man."

I scoffed, turning back to my store to leave him alone in the street. It served him right.

"When you're done," he called, "I should like to walk you home."

"Again," I tossed over my shoulder, "It's unnecessary. I happen to live upstairs."

"Oh." I could hear the smile in his voice, and I paused with my hand hovering over the door handle, waiting to hear what he had to say despite myself. "Then it will be easier to keep you safe from more sprites, you see." I pressed my lips together, anxious for our interaction to come to its end. "The renovations are complete in my apartment. I'll be above the bakery from now on."

I think I may have shrieked–grunted? I'm not sure, but I was absolutely fed up.

I grabbed the handle of the tea shop door, swinging it open so hard the bells slammed against the glass.

"Goodnight, Furious." I heard him call behind me as the door closed.

I cracked it open once more, determined to have the last word. "My name," I said a bit too forcefully, "is Isla."

And with that, I slammed the door, leaving the second bag of trash for the next night. Come tomorrow morning, I'd be happy to drag it into the closet. It would be worth the delay if it meant I didn't have to spend one more moment in the presence of Cyris the baker.

THREE

"Oh, come on Clem," I muttered to myself, rummaging around one of the counters on the second story of Clementine's shop. "You could keep this place a little more organized."

I really wasn't justified in the request. My tea shop was no better. I suppose it was one of the many reasons Clem and I had become friends. She was eccentric, over the top–*kind*. I'd like to think I had a bit of that in me, though I certainly didn't enjoy fancy clothes as much as her.

When she asked me to watch over the shop while she was gone, I don't think searching around for a specific object I could borrow was what she had in mind.

I considered the way her away message frightened me upon my arrival to be my payment. When Clementine's face flashed in front of me, and her voice echoing out from the front steps, I had been so startled I almost knocked over one of the velvet couches downstairs after entering the shop. And that's saying something. Those things are heavy.

I would know since she forced me to help her move them in.

"Yes!" My fingers wrapped around the wooden stand, careful not to lose the small bowl at the top, perfect for diffusing oils. "This is exactly what I need."

I *borrowed* a bag from downstairs to hide my gift and closed up shop, careful not to trigger Clem's unnecessarily alarming away message again.

My steps were sure as the soles of my boots tapped the cobblestones beneath them, and I made my way back to the tea shop. The sun had risen, casting Fairvein in delicious warmth and light as music floated from down the street. When I finally reached the shop, I noticed Cyris exiting the bakery.

He had traded the sharp green vest and starched button-down for something more befitting of a baker–a simple white shirt, a full apron, and his ever-present and infuriating smile.

"Morning," Cyris called, and I fought the urge to turn my nose up at him.

If my plan were to be a success, I would have to start charming him now.

I turned ever so slightly in his direction, trying to plaster my own smile on my face. The expression was tight–I knew that. I had never been good at hiding my emotions, but it would have to work.

"Good morning, Cyris," I said, clutching the bag to my chest. "Would you mind if I stopped by the bakery once you open for the day?"

I hoped my tone sounded friendly–inviting–not strategic or scheming at all.

"Of course," he responded, somewhat surprised.

He stared at me.

I stared at him.

"Perfect!" I responded a bit too brightly before turning around. The smile fell from my lips as soon as I spun, my eyes rolling as if they had a mind of their own.

"Thought any more about the competition?" he asked. "The one to be mentioned in the Queen's brochure."

I turned around. "I have," I answered honestly, my expression souring before I could think better of it. I quickly tried to redeem myself, forcing another smile to my lips.

"Hmm," Cyris said, one brow raised.

I curtsied, dipping ever so slightly before rushing back into the safety of the tea shop.

As soon as I unloaded the contents of my bag on the counter, I went to work looking for one herb in particular, noisome weed.

As soon as I opened the jar, the repugnant smell hit me, nearly knocking me out. The plant smelled, well–it smelled bad.

Perfect.

I quickly used my mortar and pestle to grind it into a fine powder, mixing it in a vial with some oil, and giving it a good shake. I would normally let something like this sit for a while, but the scent from the noisome weed was strong. I was certain it would work.

It was only after I sealed the vial that I noticed the scent lingering in the air.

"Oh, absolutely not," I muttered, grabbing my room spray from beneath the counter and spraying frantically around the shop. No reasonable number of dried herbs could cover the smell of freshly ground noisome weed, but my room spray might be able to handle it.

Once my nose only detected the faintest scent lingering in the air, I gave up on my useless task, the bells sounding on the door.

Sylvia, the sixteen-year-old who worked part-time in my shop, arrived just in time for us to open. Her nose wrinkled; her bronze skin highlighted by the dim lights of my shop.

"Good morning, Sylvia," I said, grabbing up the diffuser from Clem's store and the oil I created. "Would you mind opening the shop while I run out? I have a gift to deliver to a–" I fought for the last word. "A friend," I finished, wincing.

One brow rose on Sylvia's face. "Sure."

The forest nymph wasn't exactly *friendly*, but she was a hard worker and good company regardless. Besides, I desperately needed the help when she'd asked for a job.

I nodded once, muttering my thanks as I stomped across the street, noting the open sign on the bakery.

As soon as I walked through the door, the scent of bread and jam assaulted me, and I had to admit that it smelled good. I could admit that. Especially with the knowledge that it wouldn't last long.

Cyris moved quickly to greet me, surprised that I had kept my promise to stop by.

"Here," I said, offering up the diffuser and oil. "An apology. For the way I behaved yesterday."

He took the gift, warm fingers brushing against my own, and I fought the urge to flinch away. This man, this vile man, was still the one who released a sprite in my store yesterday. Most likely an attempt to win over the queen's opinion. I wouldn't stand for it.

"Thank you," he said, somewhat surprised.

"Of course."

And with that, I left the bakery with an unimaginable amount of joy filling my chest.

Distracted.

I was hopelessly distracted.

Sylvia and I worked through the day to serve customers, and I found myself talking with them as usual, swapping stories and secrets with anyone and everyone.

It didn't stop the way my eyes continued to drift over to the bakery across the street.

I nervously fiddled with the braid draped over my shoulder, replacing my usual bun as I leaned over the counter—my eyes fixed to the building looming across the way.

The entire day had gone by, and Cyris had yet to use my gift. It was insulting, and I had had enough.

I stomped toward the door, set on carrying myself across the street to ask the frustrating baker what his problem was. I didn't understand why anyone would receive such a wonderful gift and neglect to use it.

My hand touched the door before Sylvia's voice stopped me.

"Don't you think that'll be obvious?" she asked. "He will know something is up, Isla."

I straightened, turning back to the girl stocking herbs on the far wall. "Nothing is up," I lied.

"Oh please," she scoffed. "I could smell the noisome weed as soon as I walked into the room."

"I–" I didn't have an excuse and suddenly I regretted my decision to train my employee so well.

"Don't deny it," she interrupted. "You hate Cyris." The truth. "A shame since he could give you a few pointers when it comes to your pastries."

"Sylvia!" I didn't know why everyone was insulting my baking lately. Again, I assumed it had to be Cyris's fault. He probably used something in his baking–something that would count as cheating–something that would surely cause him to lose the queen's competition.

Sylvia chuckled, but the sound was drowned out by the yelling and complaining sounding through the street.

I turned to the window, my face lighting up like the stars in a clear sky on solstice. "Finally," I whispered before poking my head out into the street. My braid got caught on the door, and I had to detangle it before I caught a glimpse of Cyris waving a towel, trying to get the smell out of his building with the door propped open.

He looked up, his brown eyes boring into mine. *He knows,* I thought.

Of course, he knew. He would be an idiot to think it wasn't premeditated. While my baking maybe did need some work–maybe, I knew my skill with herbs couldn't be matched. It was clearly intentional.

When the smile tugged at his lips, a wicked promise of repayment, I grunted and slammed the door shut. The poor door had been abused the past few days, slamming more than any door should slam.

I leaned my back against the window, closing my eyes and gathering my thoughts.

"What just happened?" Sylvia asked, and I blew out a breath, looking up at her confused expression.

"I think," I began, "I think I just started a war."

Four

"Come *on*, you stupid thing," I grunted, tugging at the short rope attached to my new nemesis–a small goat named Myrtle. I was pulling with all my strength, certain that this goat was enchanted with some kind of magic. I was not exactly lithe and willowy, though short, I still had just enough weight on me to certainly tip the scale in my favor. This goat had to *move*.

I grunted, my behind landing right on the stone in front of the tea shop, only halfway to my destination. Throwing the rope down, I glared at the goat. "You're about as stubborn as an ass!"

Cyris's deep laugh sounded next to me, and when I turned, he was in the process of wiping tears from his eyes.

I gladly shifted my glare from goat to baker. "What is wrong with you?" I questioned.

Cyris stepped forward; his apron covered in flour from his morning baking activities. Everything about him infuriated me.

"And how is sweet Myrtle doing?" he asked, kneeling to pet the goat.

It figured the two of them would be the best of friends.

"How do you know Myrtle?" I questioned, my eyes narrowing. Something wasn't adding up.

"Oh, you know–" he began but didn't finish. Cyris just focused on rewarding my new enemy.

I brushed the dirt off my shoulder as if it would somehow take care of the dust that certainly coated my rear where I still sat on the ground, booted feet stretched out in front of me.

I offered Cyris an explanation for my encounter with the goat. "Mrs. Elwood heard about a goat for sale at the bottom of the mountain. Figured it would help her since she makes that fancy soap," I said. "She stopped by last night right before closing to ask if I would take her coin down and bring the goat up to her home. Which was exactly what I was doing before you chose to *laugh* at me." I glared at him, but Cyris didn't notice and simply continued cooing at the creature. "So, I'll ask you again, Cyris. How do you know Myrtle?"

He laughed again, a dark chuckle that skittered down my spine, causing embarrassment to flush my cheeks. "I mentioned sweet Myrtle to Mrs. Elwood yesterday after having to spontaneously close my shop." He gave me a pointed look. I pretended not to notice. "I may have suggested she ask you to help her out. You're quite generous, Isla. Everyone in town speaks of it." He stood up, offering me a hand. "I must admit, I knew about Myrtle's temperament, her owners being dear friends of mine."

I slammed my palms on the stone, pushing myself up and huffing in Cyris's direction. "How dare you," I seethed.

"How dare I?"

"You planned this on purpose."

His smile widened, brown eyes glittering in the morning light, tinted pink from the sun. Cyris scratched at his beard. "I may have had something to do with this one," he admitted.

"I knew it!" I turned around, then spun back, not really certain what I should do with my body. Maybe I was just trying to get rid of some energy.

Facing Cyris again, I waited for an apology. I still wasn't sure how I'd get the goat all the way to Mrs. Elwood's house. I *did* promise her a new goat. Maybe Clem had something in her shop to help drag stubborn animals uphill.

"I'll take care of the goat," Cyris said, causing me to pause. I blinked at him. "I need you to believe me, Isla. I didn't intentionally release the sprite."

I clenched my jaw briefly before responding. "Of course, you didn't." My tone was tight. I didn't believe him for a second.

"I didn't," he insisted. "Let me make it up to you, more than taking care of the goat catastrophe I created."

"Sure," I said, folding my arms across my chest. Sylvia walked past us, making her way into the tea shop without a word. Not an ounce of acknowledgment or aid. All hopes of getting out of this conversation early disappeared. "What did you have in mind?"

"Come over tonight after closing," he said, and something in my heart stuttered–jumped a little. I'm certain it was written on my face. "I'll give you a baking lesson."

"A baking lesson?" That vile, loathsome, demeaning, and intoler-able–

He leaned down, picking up the rope strapped to what I could only describe as a monster hidden in a goat's body. "Yes."

"Let me get this straight." My voice spewed venom. "Your idea of making it up to me involves insulting my pastries? Insinuating I need some kind of baking lesson?"

Cyris, for all it was worth, grimaced. "I can see how you came to that conclusion."

I shook my head, no longer angry but defeated.

Tired?

No. *Exhausted.*

"Just leave, Cyris. I'm tired of talking to you." I brushed a hair away from my face, watching his expression fall.

"Of course," he answered, turning to scoop up the goat as if it weighed nothing and carrying it up the hill.

I let out an exasperated breath, turning to open shop with Sylvia.

Once the store officially opened, Luna sauntered her way into the store, one of the regulars. Though, after Sylvia showed me the paper detailing the queen's plan to send people this week, I figured we would start seeing new faces soon. That, and the tourist season was about to begin.

"Good morning, Luna. How was the archery tournament last week? Did you win?"

Luna tucked a bright red strand of hair behind one pointed and pierced ear, smiling at the question. The elven woman was a phenomenal archer, and I enjoyed hearing all about her sport when she came in to get her tea.

Oh! Tea!

I quickly grabbed the dewberry blend off the shelf and began preparing her usual order.

"It was great, Isla. Though I'm starving after the long trip back from the continent." She peered into the pastry case, eyeing some of the items I baked just last night. "Those scones look good. Could I get one of those?"

"Of course!" I beamed, quickly preparing the pastry on one of my fine-painted plates, the pastel green one with wildflowers painted on it.

Sliding her tea across the counter, I watched as Luna took a bite, chewed–chewed, and grimaced.

My stomach sank.

Luna placed the scone back onto the plate before speaking. "I heard about the noisome weed oil," she chuckled, taking a long sip of tea, one much too long.

I eyed her carefully, noting that my scones were maybe not as good as I thought they were. I hadn't tried them in a long while. I wouldn't exactly *know*.

"Anyway," Luna continued, "the rumor is that you're the responsible party. Is it true?"

"Of course, it's true!" There was no point in hiding it. "The idiot released an air sprite into my shop! Destroyed everything!" I was talking with my hands, desperately trying to get Luna to side with me.

"Everything?" she questioned, cocking a brow.

My shoulders drooped. "Well, pretty much."

"Isla Alden," she said. "You are something else." She chuckled, grabbing her tea and moving to one of the tables as more customers entered.

Sylvia popped out from the back kitchen—her face expressionless. "Did you see how she left the scone on the counter," Sylvia said, and I felt the dig right in my heart.

I winced. "Cyris asked if he could give me some pointers."

"You should take him up on it." She grabbed the plate, dumping the scone in the trash before disappearing again.

Sylvia was right. I needed to work on my baking skills, but I couldn't stand the thought of allowing Cyris to be the one to help me.

He couldn't possibly help me.

Could he?

FIVE

I stood in front of the darkened bakery for at least fifteen minutes. The sun long since descended in the sky, disappearing beyond the horizon. Noises drifting from the tavern down the street kept drawing my attention, reminding me that the tourist season was starting.

It also reminded me of the queen's competition. To be featured in the brochure would have been life-changing, certainly. That kind of exposure would encourage people to stop by in droves. I liked to believe I had it in me to woo anyone entering the shop, that I would have treated all those newcomers well—given them the best tea blends in Edessa.

Maybe not the best pastries, though.

I raised my hand to knock on the door but lowered it just as quickly. Would he even be able to hear my knock from so far away? His apartment was above the bakery, and if it was anything like mine, he probably didn't have any way of knowing if someone stood down below trying to reach him. Cyris would have benefited from a door buzzer like the one Clem had given me.

I shook my head, still debating, when the door pushed open.

"I've been watching you stand there alone for the last fifteen minutes," he said, his hair significantly more mussed than I'd seen it before. Cyris wore a loose cream-colored shirt and brown linen pants, his warm eyes shining with mischief. "I wanted to make sure you weren't dropping off another stink bomb."

The chuckle escaped my lips before I could think better of it. "Your baking lesson–" I started, unable to finish the sentence.

He leaned in ever so slightly. "Yes?" he inquired.

I still wasn't looking at him, my eyes fixed well on my feet, my hands wringing in front of my navy dress. I left the apron in the tea shop, though. "It might be appealing," I admitted, raising my gaze to meet his and allowing the smirk to pull the corners of my mouth upward. "Just slightly."

Cyris didn't say anything, merely scooted backward while holding the door and gesturing for me to move indoors.

Aside from the dimly lit stairwell behind the counter, the bakery was completely dark, and something about it had nerves skating over my skin and making me jittery.

"So," I said, trying to break the uncomfortable silence while following him through the shop. "Smells nice in here."

Cyris looked over his shoulder, stepping onto the first step. "So I'm told," he replied–no malice in his tone.

I followed him to the top of the steps where the stairwell opened to his immaculate apartment. A green velvet couch stood firmly in place, just in front of a crackling fire. The room was clean, decorated with taste, and certainly cozy. Not what I expected from a cold-hearted viper.

He wasn't, though.

Cold.

Or a viper.

He was, however, responsible for ruining my morning with one very stubborn and ridiculous goat.

"This is where you live?" I asked, trying to make conversation.

He smiled, leaning his hands on the island in the middle of his kitchen space just beyond the seating area. "I assume you already know that, considering how you stood in front of my door for centuries waiting to knock."

"It was not centuries," I defended. "What do you think I am, an elf?"

"Your ears tell me you are not an elf," he chuckled. "Mortal, like me, then?"

"Not quite," I answered, moving further into the room and pulling up the linen sleeve of my dress to reveal the sun and moon branded there, the raised scar turned white with age. "A healer," I supplied.

"A healer's mark," he mused before meeting my gaze. "But you are not a healer?"

I strode to the island, tapping a finger on the wooden surface and avoiding his eye contact. Something about the way he looked at me made my skin itch. Not unpleasantly, though. "In a sense, not. I was. But owning a tea shop sounded far superior."

"As it would be." Cyris stood still, smiling when I looked up at him. There was an openness to the expression, one that told me he would answer any question I asked of him—disclose all of his secrets. Secrets were my favorite currency. I couldn't hold them, surely, but I loved to unearth them.

"And why did you move here? To Fairvein, I mean."

"The question of the hour." His tongue clicked behind his teeth before Cyris turned to gather ingredients from a cupboard. "I lived on the continent my entire life. Busy city, I guess. It was time for a change."

"And you've always wanted a bakery?" I pressed.

"Always." His features softened as he sorted the ingredients on the table and pulled out a bowl from beneath the island. "When my mother died, it seemed as good a time as any." He smiled again, but this time, it was different—filled with muted sorrow.

I nodded, letting the information wash over me. "I'm sorry," I said, and I meant it. "Was your mother's death the change you referred to? The reason you moved?"

He sighed, leaning his hands against the countertop. "I suppose it was."

We stood in comfortable silence, eyes locked and hearts beating in a way that had my skin itching again. It was difficult to hold hatred in my heart when Cyris appeared so—*vulnerable.*

I had unearthed a secret, one that felt heavier than I anticipated. His move had been a result of his mother's death. Even so, I didn't want to push anymore. Those details seemed private–intimate, even.

I settled for the companionable quiet, letting the fire crackle in the distance. I scratched at my neck just before the silence broke.

"Well," he jolted, wiping his hands on his pants. "I heard your scones are the worst. Let's start there."

"You heard what?" My voice came out louder than intended, a bit animalistic—laced with a serious threat.

"The town talks." He shrugged, still confident in his words–not knowing how badly I wanted to toss him out the window of this apartment. Or maybe possibly feed him to a griffin. "Isla," he continued, "your talent is tea, and that's just fine. Let me help you with the treats."

I huffed, moving to his side of the counter before conceding. "Fine," I muttered.

"Okay," he began, surveying the ingredients one more time. "Flour, sugar, butter." He listed them, and I followed along for the most part, infuriated because this sounded a whole like the scones I already made. "Baking powder, salt, eggs, heavy cream."

"Heavy cream?" I turned my head to face him, shock etched into every new line forming on my face. I would carry the stress lines with me into old age. His presence the last few days had caused more than I would have liked to admit.

"Oh, gods above," he chuckled. "What are you feeding your customers? Stones made from the dust in your attic?"

"My apartment doesn't have an attic."

Cyris cocked an eyebrow in my direction. "I won't believe that until I see it."

My cheeks flushed bright pink, and I looked down at the jar of flour, carefully removing the glass lid. I didn't understand the reaction or the incessant itching that reappeared with his comment. I scratched at my palm, begging the sensation to go away. "My attic?" I questioned.

"Your apartment."

Clearing my throat, I did my best to follow along with his detailed instructions and demonstrations, but I found that every time our fingers brushed, my brain short-circuited. *Utterly ridiculous,* I thought.

After deciding that our scones would be of the blueberry variety, Cyris lit the fire in the brick oven, and we gave them time to cook, talking about his new life in Fairvein and the successful goat delivery that took place earlier in the afternoon.

Once the pastries cooled, I decided I had been wrong about everything and silently thanked Sylvia for her subtle insults that pushed me to the bakery door this evening. Cyris had been right in the beginning, my scones were atrocious compared to the work of art I bit into, and it was probably because they were dry as stones made from the dust in my non-existent attic. I wouldn't know about the scones, though. I hadn't eaten them in years. That, in and of itself, said something significant.

"Thank you," I whispered to Cyris as he handed me a linen towel with our magical creations tucked tightly inside. "I don't think I can thank you enough."

"Any time." He offered a crooked smile, and we stood at the top of the stairs, gazes locked for what felt like an elven lifetime. The fire crackled in the hearth as that very same itching sensation took over again. I wondered if I would ever be able to get rid of it–what it was.

"Well," I said, shaking off the dizzying haze of our staring contest. "I should go." I scratched at my wrist.

"Let me walk you out."

"No!" My voice came out too loud and harsh. "No," I said in an attempt to soften it. "I'll be just fine. It's only across the street."

Cyris nodded, and I curtsied, quickly scrambling down the steps, out the door, across the street, and into the safety of my own building.

"Oh, Clem," I whispered to my empty apartment. I didn't dare open the curtains for fear of seeing him in the window across the way. "If only you were here to talk to."

I should hate him–I should really, really hate him, but the truth was my heart was easily won, and everyone knew it.

He had helped me tonight, and I found that whatever vexation had remained in my chest before, vanished. When he told me about his mother–his move–I almost enjoyed the conversation.

And unfortunately, even though he was across the street doing whatever the gods knew, my skin just simply would not stop itching.

Six

The tea shop and, by default, my apartment, were filled with the scent of blueberries and freshly baked scones. After my lesson with Cyris, I decided I couldn't let my new talents go to waste.

Sylvia walked in, tying her apron around her waist and removing a twig from her wavy, black hair. Deep green moss wove its way through the strands where they lay braided down her back. As soon as Sylvia made it to the counter, she paused, glancing at the case I filled with the fresh scones.

"Those smell good," she stated, eyes narrowing. "Are they your handiwork?"

"Yes," I replied with a smug smile on my face. "Cyris's recipe, though."

"May I try one?"

I set the tray down on the counter, glaring at her. Sylvia was unfazed, as usual, but it didn't stop me from communicating my immense disapproval. "That's insulting, Sylvia."

She blinked, looking once at the scones and back at me. "I figured you'd be used to my insults by now."

I huffed, sliding a small plate with delicately painted trees on its surface. It was her favorite, though the forest nymph would never admit it. In fact, I don't think she'd ever admit to liking anything. "Here," I said, placing one of the warm scones on the plate and pointedly placing it in front of her.

Despite her insult, I couldn't help the way I stared, desperately trying to decipher if the scones were–*good*. To be honest, I couldn't bring myself to try one–worried that I messed up the recipe so thoroughly I would disappoint myself with the results.

Sylvia cringed away from my gaze. "Would you stop staring?" Turning around, she bit into the pastry, and despite my fears, the tea shop did not explode upon her trying the item.

"They're good," she said, setting it back on the plate before moving into the back of the tea shop. I didn't bother giving her space, pulling a stray strand of hair back into the bun atop my head.

"Right!" I said, taking in the mess from the kitchen. "We spent the entire evening together. Cyris explained all the different variations I could create. Did you know you're supposed to use heavy cream or buttermilk with those? No wonder my old ones were so dry." I leaned against the counter as Sylvia gathered a bag of dried aline petals to replenish out in the shop. "Good call on the aline petal tea. That will get them feeling all sorts of adoration for my tea shop."

"Isla, you are ruthless." Sylvia rolled her eyes, and I followed her back out into the shop again. "You spent the entire evening with Cyris?"

My brow furrowed and my cheeks heated, the flush working up my neck and making my skin prickle and itch like it had last night. "When you say it like that Sylvia–" I trailed off, glaring at her. "Are you even old enough to make such insinuations?"

"I'm sixteen." Sylvia pulled down the jar for the petals and began restocking it. "I'm old enough to know the basics of how elves, nymphs, and mortals are made."

I saw the small tug of her full mouth, ever so subtle and indicating her complete amusement in making me uncomfortable.

Folding my arms across my chest, I shifted where I stood. "Nothing like that," I muttered before moving back to the counter to put the tray away. "Nothing of the such." Clearing my throat, I offered as many details as I could, hoping it would prove my honesty. "I stood outside the bakery for no shorter than fifty years trying to decide if I should go in. Cyris saw me and let me upstairs, where he laid out ingredients for scones. We talked about his reasons for coming to Fairvein, which were much sadder than I anticipated, though that is not my story to tell. When the scones were done, we ate them, and I left."

"Hm." Sylvia nodded once.

"You must believe me!"

She sighed, exhausted with me already. "I do, Isla." Her head tilted to the side; her expression annoyed. "I'm certain that if anything of the romantic variety happened with you and Cyris, you would have told the entire town."

I stared at her, mouth agape, as she disappeared back into the kitchens.

Leaving it alone, I flipped the sign to *open* and waited for guests to arrive.

After listening to the raucous noise from the tavern last night, I was certain that the tourist season was upon us. Late spring was here, and the shop would soon be filled with guests from all over Edessa. And of course, I couldn't forget the guests sent by the queen.

The guard had been drinking his aline petal tea blend for the last five minutes, and I was doing my best not to stare.

Even Sylvia stood next to me, nervously brushing down her apron and looking at the guard seated in the far corner of the shop. Other patrons chatted, drank, and ate delicious scones, but it seemed all of the attention couldn't help but be pulled toward the tall man in the corner, the sheer mask worn by all of the queen's guards long since removed. He had taken a bite of his scone, too. I couldn't help but wonder if he had enjoyed it.

"The queen wouldn't be so obvious as to send one of her guards?" Sylvia questioned; her gaze firmly fixed on the man.

"Stop staring. *You* are the one who is being obvious."

She huffed, turning to face me. "Must you be so obtuse? You've been staring at the same man the entire time."

"Why do you insist on insulting me at every turn?"

A throat cleared in front of the counter, both of us reeling back at the tall man now looming over us, his features severe, jawline fit to slice an agmund gem in two.

"Miss Isla?" he questioned; his gaze pinned right on me.

"Yes?" I responded.

Something softened in his features, the severe expression fleeing at the confirmation of my identity. "The scones you made? Absolutely lovely. And the tea, what did you say the blend consisted of?"

I smiled, certain that the smattering of freckles across my face lifted infinitesimally. There was no sense in lying to him about the particular tea blends. Most wouldn't recognize the name unless they one, worked in the tea shop with me, or two, were a healer themselves.

"Aline petals," I answered. "I blend the flower petals with other dried herbs and add in berries for a hint of sweetness."

"Is that right?" A smile stretched across his face as he casually leaned over the counter, elbows hitting the surface. Somehow, that kept him at eye level with me.

He was quite handsome, this guard. Though his resting expression appeared harsh, when he spoke to you, you hardly remembered that.

"I know quite a lot about herbs and plants, being a former healer," I offered. "It's one of the reasons I wanted to open a tea shop." The smile remained on his face, and I found that it wasn't at all unpleasant.

Sylvia huffed and moved around the counter, opening the door for whatever guest just arrived. I was happy to leave her to it.

"You know," I said, "I noticed you're one of the queen's guards. What is it that has you coming all the way out here to Fairvein?"

"Well," he said, leaning in as if he were offering me the most delicious secret. "The queen is set to arrive in a few days. It should be announced in the paper soon. I'm here to prepare the castle and test out the shops."

"Test out the shops?" My brows rose, and I couldn't help the way the excitement seeped into my tone.

He chuckled, a knowing laugh that lingered in my ears long after the sound ceased. "Yours happens to be one of the best. I was wondering." His gaze met mine, warming just enough to let me see the interest behind it. "I would love to spend more time here. Is there a time of day when the tea shop is slower? Possibly a moment we could sit together and talk? I'd love to hear about your passion for your store."

My heart soared in my chest, the reality of what was happening crashing into me like a dragon smashing through a building. "Of course!"

"Isla," Cyris's voice interrupted the intimate conversation, and the guard immediately stood up, the severe expression returning to his face.

Cyris was shorter, though still taller than me. He looked up at the guard once and nodded before turning in my direction. He casually placed a hand on the counter, leaning in a way that said he frequented the shop–and conversations with me.

"The scones seem to be going well," he said, a wide smile stretching across his face. "Have you told everyone you spent the entire night over at my apartment learning to make them with me? Have I put myself out of business?"

A flush worked up my neck. "I may have mentioned our completely *platonic* meeting to Sylvia."

One brow rose on Cyris's handsome and infuriating face. "Platonic?" he questioned.

"Excuse me," the guard said, turning to return to his seat, and I grunted–loudly.

"Are you trying to make me lose my spot in the queen's travel brochure?" My voice was caught somewhere between a frustrated yell and a whisper.

Cyris matched my expression, leaning in, the smile dropping away from his face. It was strange to see him so serious. "No," he answered–confident as ever. "It wasn't about that. That guard–" I couldn't help the way my eyes flicked behind Cyris to the man now seated by the window. "That guard was flirting with you, Isla."

I shrieked as quietly as possible, so I wouldn't draw attention to our tense conversation. "Maybe I liked being flirted with," I offered. "I *do* enjoy the attention."

Cyris rolled his eyes. "Oh, please." I'd never seen the man lose his casual charm, the easygoing smile, and amusement completely fleeing in the wake of his irritation. "I've tried that," he said, gesturing to me. "You hardly enjoyed the experience of flirting with me."

My mouth hung open, his voice just a little too loud for my liking. People from all over the shop were staring at us, and it made my stomach twist and churn. My skin ignited and itched more than it ever had before. Had he admitted to–

"Don't look at me like that," Cyris said, and I fought to keep my composure, though it was a useless endeavor.

His eyes were so focused on me, taking in my face, my freckles, the wild hair atop my head. Suddenly, the room felt incredibly hot, and I was certain I had been coming down with some rare rash–the way my body flushed and prickled all over.

Could he tell?

While I found myself not completely opposed to the idea of Cyris flirting with me–or looking at me the way he was, for that matter–I couldn't shy away from the reality of what he had just done. The queen's guard had come to enjoy the shop, sent to scope out the stores here in Fairvein. He had to be here for the brochure, and Cyris may have just thwarted my chances at a feature.

"You should hope you didn't ruin this for me, Cyris. I will never forgive you if you did."

"I find that hard to believe." His casual amusement returned, and it bore with it all the previously experienced exasperation I had felt toward him.

"Oh, just go back to the bakery." My body was still too warm from what he said. I needed room to breathe, and time to woo the man still sitting in the corner, staring at us.

Cyris muttered something under his breath, turning to saunter across the room, looking once at the guard before opening the door.

"This is war, Cyris Buford!" I called from my comfortable position at the counter.

He waved me off, looking back once over his shoulder before retreating into his own store.

"You two are the most exhausting creatures I have ever seen." In the time Cyris had exited, Sylvia had sidled up next to me, set on spouting her opinions. "You're lucky Clementine isn't here to witness it."

I twisted to look at her. "Why do you say that?" I asked. Clementine had been gone for a number of days, and while I didn't know much about the adventure she had gone on–something about a rare item she needed to find, a great reward–I certainly missed her, dearly.

Sylvia chuckled; a sound so rare I wasn't sure she had actually done it. "She'd fill the two of you with wine and sweets on the couches in that shop of hers. It would all be in the hopes of inspiring a grand love story. That woman does love to romanticize life, and I must admit, I see the potential."

I rolled my eyes. "What do you know," I said, turning away to fiddle with the jars on the wall behind the counter. "You're sixteen."

Sylvia merely shook her head, making her way back into the kitchen to tend to the kettle.

SEVEN

The sunlight had disappeared over Fairvein, but I still found it difficult to see the stars. With the tourist season underway, every lantern in the street had been lit, the lamps flickering and polluting the darkness.

I sighed, resting the final trash bag against the side of my shop, ready for the trash goblin's nightly pickup. Taking one last look at the bakery, my heart sank.

There was a small part of me that wanted to run into Cyris again, and though I didn't want to read into those feelings much, they were still there.

Walking back into the shop, I halted at the dark figure looming over the counter, flipping through the pages of my herbal manual. My heart tipped toward the line of *too fast*, and I clutched the sides of my beige, linen dress–ready to make a run for it. Good thing I chose to wear my boots.

It was then that I noticed who the man was.

The queen's guard.

"Oh, it's you," I breathed, my heart failing to slow enough for me to get my bearings.

The book snapped shut in his large hand, and I jolted. Something about his presence here in my dark tea shop made me uncomfortable, no matter how charming he had been earlier.

"What were you looking for?" I asked, laughing nervously. "Also, when you mentioned coming to the shop," I continued, "I thought you meant while we were still open." My brow furrowed, but I quickly corrected it with a soft smile. "You said as much, anyway." I nearly added that it was good to see him, but based on the way my stomach churned, I decided against it.

He hadn't said anything, the sheer mask still covering part of his face.

"You're in town as a scout for the brochure, right?" I couldn't help the way my voice shook ever so slightly. My attempt at determining his reasoning for entering my shop was apparent.

"More or less," he said, but there was no smile on his lips–none that I could see–even after he removed the mask. "I wanted to buy something in particular from you," he stated, setting the book on the counter and striding closer. "Official business of the queen."

"Oh." My eyes flicked to the door, wondering how he had gotten in here to begin with. "Okay."

"You can see why I had to wait for your shop to close." The smile that broke across his face was nothing like the one from earlier. This one reminded me of a viper ready to strike. "Do you have dried Eleri?" he asked. "The herb."

I blinked, my nose scrunching briefly. What on earth did he need dried Eliri for? "Yes," I said. "But that is not an herb suited for tea. It's quite poisonous once ingested. That herb is better used in salves for minor cuts and scrapes." My hope was that giving him more information would deter him from asking for the herb again. Something wasn't sitting right. "I don't typically sell the dried herb," I stated plainly enough. "Just the salve."

"Ah," he said, moving closer, and I took a step back. "I'm in need of the herb, you see." His hand rested on the sword strapped to his belt, and my eyes flicked to the weapon briefly, the hairs raising on my neck. "Again, it's at the queen's request."

I stared at him, trying to detect the lie. He *was* a guard. He did work for the queen. It wasn't abnormal for the royals to show up needing something they didn't want the public to know about. The royal family, the Cranefields, were beloved in the kingdom. I thought that maybe I was feeling nervous for no reason. Maybe it was all in my head.

"Of course," I said. "I can package that up for you."

Moving back to the small room behind the kitchen where I kept more dangerous herbs, I worked quickly to fill a small bag with the Eliri herb, careful not to spill or mix it into anything else. The guard had been so charming earlier, I couldn't imagine a reason for such a shift. It very well could have been the darkness making me nervous. Everything seemed scarier once the sun disappeared beyond the horizon.

"Here you go," I said, handing him the bag after returning to the front of the shop.

"Thank you, Miss Isla," he said, bowing ever so slightly and holding the smile in place on his face.

"Of course."

He stepped forward again, crowding my space, and I fought the urge to reel back. "And I'll put in the good word for you and the shop." He smiled again, his white teeth shining in the dim light of the one lantern along the far wall. "For the travel brochure, you see."

I didn't respond, the air fleeing my lungs as we stared at one another. I couldn't stop the way my palms were sweating, fiddling with the skirts of my dress. I very much wanted him to leave.

Just then, the bells on the door sounded, and Cyris walked through the entrance, gaze cast down toward his feet, his hair mussed atop his head as if he had been pulling at the strands relentlessly. "Isla," he said, determined. "I've come to apologize. I just couldn't-" He stopped abruptly, his eyes taking in the scene before him. With brows furrowed, he continued talking, changing his trajectory. "I'm sorry to interrupt," he said, eyes flicking between us. "I will come back later."

"No!" I said, my voice a bit too loud, and the guard's gaze slid my way. "No, no. It's quite alright, Cyris. I was expecting you anyway." I tried to tell him everything I couldn't say aloud with the expression on my face, hoping he would read me well. "The baking lesson, and all."

"Oh," his eyes flicked between us again, my words registering and hitting the mark. "Yes, of course. I apologize for being a bit early." He let out a casual laugh, and I was thankful for the way he could seem so at ease.

"It's quite alright," I responded.

The guard grunted, muttering his thanks and exiting out the front door, the bells jingling behind him.

Cyris moved to stand next to me, his arm brushing against my own, and I found comfort in that small point of contact.

"What was that about?" he asked, tone serious.

"Nothing good, to be sure," I said, folding my arms across my chest. The gesture wasn't relaxed–more a way to protect myself from the uncomfortable feelings as best I could. "Though I don't have a real reason for why the experience was so unsettling."

We continued staring out into the now empty street, the presence of the guard still lingering in the night.

"Sometimes," Cyris began, "sometimes the feeling is reason enough. Did you let him in here?"

I shook my head, turning to face him. Warm brown eyes traced my features, searching and worried. His gaze brought me comfort, too.

"No," I answered honestly. "I was taking out the trash and came back inside. He had just appeared."

"Through the back door then?"

A chill worked down my spine. It was the only explanation for the guard's abrupt arrival–the way he snuck into my shop without alerting me. "Must have been."

Cyris grunted, looking once at the door before turning back. "I don't like that. I don't like that at all."

I had to admit I didn't like it either, but he *did* work for the queen. Unsettling or not, he had to be at least a bit trustworthy. "He does work for the royal family. I'm sure I was just being ridiculous." The nervous laugh I released didn't do much to support my point. It only served to make Cyris's expression even more serious.

"No, you are not being ridiculous, Isla." Cyris took a step closer, his proximity soothing as opposed to whatever reaction the guard's proximity brought. "Listen, this may be a bit forward," he started. "Especially with what happened earlier between us, but I think you should stay with me." His eyes softened–pleading. "At least for tonight."

Worry wove its way into my blood, tightening my chest. "And leave the shop after *that*?" There was no way I could leave. The guard knew where the dangerous herbs were. He had to. "Cyris, I can't."

"Fine," he said, insistent. "Then let me stay here. You will hardly notice my presence."

My eyes roamed around the room, searching for a reason to say no. "I don't know."

"Isla." My name on his lips drew my attention, my eyes locking with his. Cyris reached up and brushed a strand of hair gently behind my ear, the touch buzzing over my skin long after his hand had fallen away. "Please," he begged. "Let me protect you, my dear Furious. It would make me feel the most noble."

"I told you not to call me that," I said, but I couldn't stop the grin from appearing on my face.

Cyris let out a breathy laugh. "Right, of course. I must have forgotten."

I didn't believe him for a moment. "Well," I said. "Go get your things, then. I suppose you can stay." As soon as the words left my lips, his face lit up. "I was just about to lock up."

"Yes, yes." Cyris began moving, a bit flustered, and I had to admit, it was a funny sight. "I'll be back," he said. "When I get here, do let me in, or else I'll be hopelessly disappointed."

I laughed again, watching him open the door with my hip resting on the counter and my arms folded across my chest. I couldn't help the way my cheeks turned pink, my chest warming at his gesture. "Don't worry, Cyris," I said. "I'll let you in."

EIGHT

I fluffed the pillow before dropping it onto the beige couch in the center of the apartment, Cyris's presence a constant reminder of where he would be sleeping tonight.

After the event with the guard, I didn't mind him staying here, though I was nervous for some reason. It wasn't the uneasy feeling from earlier, but something that had my mind buzzing despite the silence in the room.

I draped the blanket over the arm as the fire crackled in the hearth and looked at my handiwork. My apartment was small, quaint with books and trinkets decorating every corner—a symptom of my friendship with Clem, no doubt. The dried herbs hanging from the ceiling reminded me of my tea shop below. The warmth felt like home.

Cyris cleared his throat behind me. "So," he began, "you decided to give up your position as healer to own a tea shop in Fairvein?"

He was fishing for information, just as I had done with him in his own apartment. Luckily enough, I didn't mind talking about myself. Not in the slightest.

"Yes," I said, turning to him. "I did."

"Why?" he asked, and I could have predicted the question like some sort of oracle. He was certainly looking for information. That, or he was simply trying to get to know me.

"It's a long story," I said, pulling the socks higher up my calf. In the time he had spent donning his own night clothes, I had put on my long nightgown and socks, braiding my hair and tying it off with a ribbon. "I'm sure you know the healers in Edessa descended from a long line of witches," I said. "While the magic in that line has weakened, it's still there." I ran my fingers over the sleeve of my nightgown, feeling the raised brand on my arm. "The healers all over the country use herbs and other resources for medicinal purposes, but there's also a little something else to it."

"Magic?" he guessed.

I gave him a tight-lipped smile, one that showed exactly how uncomfortable this story was. Not because I didn't want to share it but because of the truth of it. The truth about me. My deficiencies. "Magic," I affirmed. "To put it quite plainly, I don't exactly have the little extra. Not enough of it to make a difference, anyway."

"I see." He nodded thoughtfully before moving to sit on the couch. I took that as my cue to move to my bed across the room. It didn't feel quite far enough, not when his presence made that ridiculous and invisible rash reappear. "You have no magic."

It wasn't rude—the way he said it, simply stating a fact, and I had long since dealt with my feelings on the matter.

I crawled into bed, pulling the quilt over my body and leaning back on the pillows. "Not like my mother." I cleared my throat and heard Cyris settle himself on the couch. "In fact, it was quite disappointing for her," I admitted. "I moved here when I was sixteen. That was eight years ago, and I haven't looked back."

"That is—" Cyris paused, no doubt deciding how to respond. It wasn't new news. In fact, I was a little befuddled as to why he hadn't heard the story from the townsfolk already. Fairvein was known for its gossip. He certainly knew about the dire state of my pastries. "That's sad," he finished.

I chuckled, noting the caution in his response. It wasn't needed. "I love it here," I offered. "And I love my shop, too, so it's not as sad as it seems." I closed my eyes, thinking about the store below, how nice it would be to win the queen's feature in her brochure. It was all I could ever hope for. "Maybe that's why I gave Sylvia the job. She reminds me a lot of myself." My brows furrowed, my eyes fixed firmly to the ceiling. "Well, she's grumpier. Certainly quieter. The nymph has less of a filter, too. Far prettier, I can see that already." I laughed again, realizing that I had been quite wrong in my reasoning. "Maybe she's nothing like me at all. It was only her age that persuaded me."

Cyris's smokey laugh sent my skin buzzing, suddenly making the room feel far too hot. I should have taken off my socks, instead.

Silence hung in the air, and I found myself settling more and more. Sleep wouldn't be as difficult as I had previously believed. I didn't mind Cyris's presence, and it certainly helped me feel more secure. I didn't think anyone would be breaking into my apartment tonight.

"To be clear, Isla," he said, interrupting my thoughts. Cyris's voice was quiet, almost a whisper. "You are quite pretty yourself–beautiful, even." I couldn't help the way my chest warmed at his words. "The most stunning creature I've ever beheld."

I blushed, certain that the color staining my cheeks deepened far beyond pink–probably closer to a crimson red. "Thank you," I whispered, unsure of how to respond. "You're not so bad looking yourself."

He chuckled again, allowing a brief, companionable silence to stretch between us before continuing. "And as it pertains to your mother's opinions of you," he started up again, "they are complete garbage. Best to leave them out in the street for the trash goblins."

I chuckled at that. "While some of the elves on the continent may believe you are *less* for not possessing powerful magic, or whatever it is they believe they have that makes them so special, I don't believe that to be true at all." His tone turned serious as if he were speaking the most profound truth. He said it with such confidence I was inclined to believe him. "Your kindness," he said, "your willingness to help others, your vibrant personality, even the way you display your emotions so plainly–all of those things are just as valuable as magic, Isla."

His words stunned me to silence. It was a far weightier compliment than merely calling me pretty or beautiful. And while I had long since dealt with the disappointment myself, his words didn't hurt. They were like a salve used to diminish a nasty lingering scar. And for all it was worth, that salve was quite effective.

I found myself pondering the past, remembering the harsh tones my mother took with me, the demands I simply couldn't meet. I hadn't lied to Cyris, didn't see reason to. I liked my life here in Fairvein, and I was excited about the opportunity to be in the queen's brochure.

What I hadn't expected were the feelings slowly creeping into my heart–the ones that told me I would quite like to spend more time in the baker's presence.

I closed my eyes, picturing his crooked and easy smile, the wire-frame glasses that sat on his straight nose. I wondered what his lips would feel like if I brushed my finger lightly over them.

Cyris cleared his throat again, and I reined in my thoughts, acknowledging his presence in my apartment. It would be disrespectful to think about his lips now.

"Goodnight, Cyris," I said into the darkness, listening to the cool spring breeze outside the window–the fire still crackling away.

"Goodnight," he said. "My dear Furious."

Nine

The morning light floated through the window of my apartment, the orange tint casting my books and trinkets in the glorious hue. I could hear Cyris breathing from the couch, and I sat up, rubbing my eyes and thinking of the night before.

The sound of bells reached my ears, and whether it floated in from the window or up from the stairwell, I knew Sylvia had arrived to open the shop.

Sylvia!

I threw off the floral quilt, realizing how late the hour must have been. Throwing a pillow at Cyris, I quickly gathered my clothes for the day and scrambled to–there was no place to scramble too.

"Cyris, wake up. It's far too late," I said, urgency thick in my voice. "Sylvia is downstairs to open the shop, and you have a bakery to tend to."

Cyris sat upright, his brow furrowing as he watched me scramble around the open apartment, looking for a place to hide and dress. "It will be quite alright," he said, far too calmly for my liking. "One of the Andrel's kids, you know, the blacksmiths, he started helping out at the bakery. I'm sure he can handle it. I'll just dress and head over there now."

I tucked myself behind the curtain covering my closet, struggling in the cramped quarters to strip off my nightgown and pull on my sage dress for the day, making sure all my skirts were in order, and tying an apron around my waist.

When I finally emerged, Cyris was fully dressed, folding a blanket delicately over the couch.

"How are you going to leave?" I asked–frantic.

"Well," he said, "by the door, I imagine."

"Sylvia will see you!"

"So?"

I grunted, stomping my foot and turning to grab a bundle of lavender from its place on the ceiling. We were running out downstairs, and I would need to restock the jar sometime today. "You don't get it," I huffed.

Cyris's brows creased. "Are you embarrassed to be seen with me?" he asked.

I turned to him, squaring my shoulders. "No, it's not that. It's just–" I didn't know how to say it without turning the conversation into uncomfortable territory. "This looks odd, don't you think?" I cocked my head to the side, waiting for his slow–painfully slow–mind to catch up.

"Ah," he said through a laugh. "So, it's the appearance of having a man leave your apartment early in the morning." Cyris scratched at his beard. "Just tell them the truth."

"The truth," I asserted, "is completely beside the point."

"I believe you are wrong, my dear Furious." Cyris held up a finger, and something about how he didn't find this as disastrous as I did irked me. "It is *exactly* the point."

I waved him off, cradling the lavender in my arm as I shooed him down the stairwell. "Well," I said from behind him, pushing him onward. I would deliver his things promptly after the day ended. "It can't be helped, now."

When we arrived at the base of the stairs, Sylvia was standing in the kitchen, kettle in hand, and a teacup filling, filling—overflowing.

She cursed, shaking the hot water from her flesh and dunking her hand into a bucket.

"Good morning, Sylvia," Cyris said–far too chipper for my liking.

I continued shoving him out the door, trying to speak loudly enough for everyone in all of Fairvein to hear. "Thank you so much for your kindness, Cyris." *No, that sounds terrible!* I thought. "You were very sweet in sleeping very, *very* far away from me on the couch after I had that scare with an intruder last night. Really noble of you. The noblest really. I'd say you were a perfect gentleman."

Without any more acknowledgment than my frantic recounting of what had *actually* occurred, I ushered the baker out of my shop and promptly slammed the door–wincing, because the harsh treatment of the door hadn't been intentional this time.

"So," Sylvia said, a wide smile on her face. I didn't think I had seen a smile like that on the nymph in my entire time of knowing her.

I pointed at her, hoping my finger would somehow force her to listen much more fervently. "It is not what you think," I said.

"Oh?" She cocked an eyebrow. "And what is it that I think, Isla?"

"Something far too mature for you, that is to be sure," I grunted, detangling my hair as best I could with my fingers and throwing it into a wild bun atop my head.

Sylvia chuckled as she grabbed the lavender off the counter, moving the bundle back to the kitchen as she hummed happily.

"You're behaving strangely," I shouted.

She didn't waste time before shouting back. "Speak for yourself, you crazy witch!"

After my chaotic morning, I managed to find myself returning to a normal pace. The shop filled up quickly, new visitors, tourists, no doubt, arrived one after the other, and Sylvia and I were lost in our work, hardly able to think about the earlier events.

"Good afternoon!" I called to a short man as he entered the tearoom. He smiled when he glanced around the store, holding a box from Cyris's bakery in his hands.

"Good afternoon," he responded, tipping his hat toward me. "I'm here to scout the businesses in Fairvein for the queen. Just finished stopping by the bakery. Lovely jam," he said, and I found myself smiling, wiping my hands over my apron to get rid of the sweat forming on my palms. To be sure, I had become nervous all over again.

"Is it typical for you to announce who you are? I thought the scouting would be more–" I waved my hand in the air. "Discrete," I finished.

"No, no," he said, "we typically announce why we are here. I find it gives us the best service." The man winked, setting the box down on the counter and peering into the glass case filled with freshly baked scones. "What do you recommend?" he asked.

I smiled at Sylvia, and she rolled her dark eyes.

"Have you ever heard of aline petals? We have a great tea blend that incorporates the flower." I tapped my finger on the counter, waiting for his response.

"I have not. If you recommend it, I'm sure it's wonderful. Word from the young man at the bakery was that you make the best tea blends." He smiled wide, and I fought the strange flutter in my belly at the mention of Cyris's compliment. "He also mentioned something about a way with goats? Not sure what that was about."

My face fell. It would be just like Cyris to insult me without actually insulting me.

"Cyris is quite the baker," I said, moving to scoop out some of the tea blend for a fresh pot. "He's a newcomer here in Fairvein. Very kind."

"Very, *very* kind," Sylvia said from her spot at the other end of the store.

I glared at her.

"I could see that," the man said, taking his place at one of the tables. Many of the customers had turned to look in his direction, especially the locals who knew about the travel brochure.

Once he was settled with his cup in hand, I eyed the man carefully, lost in thought.

"What is it?" Sylvia asked, her voice low as she moved to stand next to me.

"I was just thinking," I said, something pulling at the pit of my belly. "If that man was sent as a scout—"

My words trailed off as Sylvia tapped the counter with her finger. I looked down to note her moss-colored nails, the ones that matched the forest she was a part of.

"You're wondering about the guard," she finished for me.

I sighed. "Yeah."

I had told Sylvia what happened last night, trusting her to hold on to his strange request like the most precious secret. She was far better at keeping those than myself, so I didn't think twice about letting her know. Plus, I wasn't sure if the guard would reappear, asking her for any more dangerous herbs. If he did, I had told her to deny him—at least until I returned.

"I don't like it," she said. "Something doesn't sit right."

"It certainly doesn't."

We watched the scout enjoy one of the scones, sipping on his tea and looking quite content where he sat, staring out the window showcasing the busy street beyond.

I wanted to be thinking about the brochure–wanted with everything in my soul to hope for the best.

Instead, I found myself distracted and ill at ease with the events of the prior day. Maybe Cyris was right in coming to stay in my apartment, regardless of what the rest of the town would think. It certainly made me feel safer.

TEN

When I found my way to the front of the store the following morning, the town buzzed with excitement. I could feel it in the way tourists and townsfolk whispered excitedly with one another–the way crowds seemed to push through the street, looking for anyone and everyone they could relay the news to.

"Did you hear?" Cyris's voice startled me, sounding so close to my ear, I was scared of turning his direction, certain I would accidentally bump my nose with his, possibly knocking the glasses off his perfect face. We couldn't have that.

"No, I didn't," I said, rolling my tongue along my cheek. Plums and cinnamon made their way to my nostrils, and I wondered if it weren't just the baking. Maybe Cyris just smelled like that. The scent was rather pleasant–not stupid at all.

"The queen arrived this morning."

I turned to him then, green eyes wide and heart fluttering with excitement. "To be sure?"

"I wouldn't lie to you, Furious."

I huffed before squeezing my lips together in a tight line, carefully brushing the flour and herbs off my apron. I had tried out a new scone recipe, hoping it would impress the same way Cyris's recipe had the past few days. "Please stop calling me that," I said before looking up.

Cyris's crooked smile sent my heart beating faster, the air far warmer than it had been mere moments ago. "I'm inclined to believe you quite like it."

"You believe wrongly."

He raised a brow, his voice smooth as he spoke, dropping to a deeper octave–one that made my mind dizzy with the sound. "Do I, now?"

Mrs. Elwood pushed her way through the crowd toward us, her silver hair pulled back to reveal pointed ears. "Have you checked your mailboxes, dears?"

"No, Mrs. Elwood," Cyris said, his voice returning to its normal cadence. "I haven't yet. Is there something worth reading?"

"I heard," she said, a bit breathlessly, "the queen is set to have a ball tomorrow night. She's invited the shop owners in Fairvein to attend at the palace. It's to announce the winners for the travel brochure."

"Already?" I asked, somewhat shocked at the swiftness of the queen's decision. Excitement raced through my blood, and hope fluttered like wings in my belly. It would surely be an accomplishment to win, and I sincerely hoped the scout who stopped by the previous day enjoyed himself.

"Check your box," Mrs. Elwood said, patting my cheek. "It is quite fast, but she's the queen. She can do as she pleases, and I'm certain you will be featured." Mrs. Elwood turned to Cyris, offering him a sweet smile. "You too, Mr. Cyris."

Cyris chuckled, and the sound had my breath catching in my throat. I did my best to hide it, however. "I'm certain only one of us can win," Cyris provided.

"Again," Mrs. Elwood said, "she is the queen. She can do as she likes."

The elven woman left us there, standing in the street with whispers of the ball surrounding us. No wonder everyone was so excited. The queen's arrival was a big deal, but the ball–it would be the first I'd heard of it in all my time living in Fairvein.

"Well then," Cyris said, breaking my thoughts. "There is to be a ball."

He smiled at me, brown eyes warm and inviting. I fiddled with the apron tied around my waist, hoping it would give me something to do, not sure of why I had become so nervous. I couldn't look at him anymore–not when he stared at me so intensely.

"Do you have a date?" he asked.

My eyes flicked back up, aghast. "I only just heard about it!" I said, far louder than I intended to. "I haven't even checked my mailbox for an official invitation."

"Of course." The smile didn't drop from his lips. "I only ask because I'm competing against the entire town."

"For a feature in the brochure?" My brows creased. "Surely you know it's all divided up into categories. The whole town is *not* your competition for the feature."

"But they are, however, my competition in securing a lovely date to the ball." He stood close–far too close.

"I'm sure you'll have no problems asking one of the fine women or elves to–"

"Furious," he said, somewhat annoyed with my ramblings. "I am asking *you*."

My heart jumped, and even though I knew what he was saying, I needed to confirm he meant it. Or maybe I just wanted to hear him speak the words aloud. "Asking me what?" I asked.

"I'm asking you to be my date, Isla. Would you attend the ball with me? You said with your own beautiful mouth that you found me handsome."

My cheeks flushed scarlet. "I did not."

"You certainly did." He placed a finger beneath my chin, forcing me to look into his eyes. "You said it only the other night."

I rolled my eyes in mock annoyance. "I did *not* call you handsome," I stated. "I recall saying the words 'you're not so bad looking yourself.'"

"Same thing." Cyris continued staring at me, waiting. "An answer," he finally insisted.

I allowed the smile to crack across my face, somewhat giddy about what he was asking me. "Okay," I said. "I will go with you."

"Wonderful!" Cyris moved quick as dragon fire, planting a kiss right on my cheek, decorating my freckles with the most precious of memories. "I will pick you up tomorrow night. Don't forget to check your mailbox. If you didn't receive your invitation, I will have to take it up with the queen."

I chuckled, running my fingers over the spot he had kissed as Cyris retreated to the bakery. "I will check," I called after him, quite content with the events of the morning so far.

Eleven

"My breasts are practically spilling out of this gown, Sylvia!" I looked down at the crimson dress. The neckline split right down the middle, nearly to my navel. While the dramatic skirts flowed outward in a way that hid my legs quite well beneath no less than forty pounds of fabric, the top was entirely too scandalous.

Sylvia sat on the chaise in Clementine's closet, laughing behind her hand. I glared at her.

"Actually, Isla," she said. "Your breasts are not *practically* spilling out of that gown. They are most certainly spilling out."

I gathered up the skirts, lifting them far easier than I should have. I attributed my strength to the muscles I had built trying to drag Myrtle up the hill to Mrs. Elwood's house. Huffing as I made my way to the rest of the hanging dresses, I looked through them once more, desperately trying to find something that would work for tonight.

Clem's taste in ball gowns was quite eccentric. Actually, her taste in anything fit that descriptor quite nicely.

I tried to navigate my way through purple, pink, floral, lace, bright—all the things I couldn't see myself wearing. I knew I was being crazy, and forcing Sylvia to come and help me into gowns wasn't exactly the right thing to do, but I *was* paying her—possibly for friendship.

"This is no use," I said, sliding my back down against the fabric behind me until I landed on the floor, staring at Sylvia seated across from me. I wished Clem were here to help. "I'm going to have to visit Julia and buy something." I looked up at the ceiling, praying to whoever would listen. "It's going to be so expensive."

Leaning back, I rested my head against the dresses behind me, letting them keep me upright. Slowly, ever so slowly at first, and then rather quickly, I fell backward between the fabric, knocking my head on the corner of a stiff cardboard box. Working my way up, which proved quite difficult in a corseted gown, I reached and dragged the box out from its hiding place and rested it on my lap.

A pretty bow sat squarely in the middle, a small note with my name carefully scrawled in cursive tucked beneath the ribbon.

"Clem is a genius."

"Really?" Sylvia questioned. "I just thought the two of you were rather crazy, to be honest. Genius wasn't the word that came to mind."

In case you ever need it.
-Clem

"We might be crazy," I said, "but you still enjoy our company." I untied the ribbon, ignoring the way Sylvia rolled her dark eyes at me.

"I don't know if you know this," she said, "but you're currently paying me to be a stand-in friend. I'm also quite a bit younger. It's rather sad."

I waved a hand. "Oh, don't be daft. I've never discriminated based on age." Carefully opening the box, I got the sense it would be exactly what I was looking for. "Well, that's not entirely true," I continued. "I do discriminate when it comes to romantic partners. I'm crazy, not disgusting."

Sylvia chuckled, betraying her previously elaborate performance set on communicating that she didn't enjoy spending time with me as much as she did.

When the box opened, I was greeted with a sage dress–tulle skirts, delicate floral bodice, all the same, glorious color. I plucked at the thin straps of the gown, noting that the neckline would be far more suited for a ball hosted by the queen of Edessa.

"It's perfect," I breathed.

"Does this mean I can go home now?"

I glared at Sylvia, lowering the gown to make sure she could see my hardened gaze. "Not yet," I said. "You'll need to help me into the dress."

"Of course." The nymph dragged herself from the chair, taking the dress from me and waving her hands in my direction. "Go on," she said. "Take off Clementine's *lady of the night gown*. Let's get this over with."

I stood up with somewhat of a struggle and began untying the bodice of the crimson dress.

When the sage gown was finally secured, looking just as stunning as I imagined, Sylvia smiled–genuinely.

"You look beautiful, Isla," she said, and my heart swelled in my chest. "Cyris is going to drop dead."

The smile on my face grew just slightly. "That is the goal, isn't it?" I looked the girl over, recalling the invitation tucked away in my apartment. "Okay," I began, "your turn."

"What?" Sylvia's eyes widened as she took a step back.

"Exactly what I said."

"I'm not a shop owner," Sylvia insisted. "I don't have an invitation."

"Funny story," I said, leaning in ever so slightly. "Employees are welcome as well. It's going to be quite the party."

"I can't."

"You *must*." I pushed her toward the dresses, noting the subtle curl to her full lips, the one that told me Sylvia didn't mind the idea of attending the ball one bit.

"Will I need to attend with you?" she asked, looking at me over her shoulder.

I shook my head. "You're safe from me for the night," I answered. "Besides." I paused before finishing my sentence. "I have a date."

TWELVE

Sylvia finished placing the last flower into my long braid before step-ping back to take in my ensemble.

"Well?" I asked, the nerves fluttering in my stomach. I would have liked to believe the nerves were due to my being invited to the queen's ball, but instead, I knew that wasn't the whole truth. It had to do with the date I would bring.

"Magnificent," she said, and she didn't appear even the slightest bit annoyed. The red dress she wore complimented her bronze skin and dark eyes, far more modest than the crimson gown I had tried on earlier.

A knock sounded on the bakery door just beyond the kitchen where we stood, and I jolted, hearing Cyris's voice float through the shop.

"Hello?"

"He's here," I whispered, wringing my hands together as Sylvia rolled her eyes, her annoyance returning in full force.

"Go," she said, reaching down to pull on her slippers. "I'll see you later at the celebration."

I nodded once before making my way to the front of the shop. Cyris wore a black suit with delicate embroidery around the cuffs and vest. His brown eyes locked onto my dress, and I fisted my hands in the skirt nervously. He looked handsome tonight–unbelievably so.

"As I said before," he said, stepping closer, "the most stunning creature I've ever beheld."

My cheeks flushed as I grabbed the dusty blue cloak from the counter. Clementine had gifted it to me a while back. There was nothing magical about this object other than the delicate flowers embroidered on the hood.

I pulled it over my shoulders, moving to tie the front when Cyris's fingers brushed against my own, sending a jolt of electricity over my skin. He made quick work of tying the ribbon, a wide smile stretching across his face.

"Are you ready?"

I met his smile with one of my own. "Absolutely," I whispered.

We made our way out into the street, walking up the cobblestone streets to the castle at the top of the town. Despite the streetlamps lining our way, the stars were out in full force, glittering despite the light surrounding us. It was as if they had brightened just for tonight.

"There have been whispers in town," Cyris said, breaking the silence as he nudged my shoulder with his own. The touch made my skin burn hot, my heart warming right along with it.

"About?" My eyes slid to him, taking in the smirk on his face.

"Us," he supplied.

I chuckled, pulling the cloak tighter around my body to keep out the cold. Despite summer's fast approach, the spring breeze still brought a light chill with it. "I did shove you out of my apartment," I started. "Quite publicly, if I remember correctly. It was all bound to draw attention eventually."

"And that it did," he said, tucking his hands into his pockets.

The silence stretched on again, comfortable and quiet just like the tea shop right before opening. It brought with it a certain peace, one that left room for dreams and wonders.

"Listen, Isla," Cyris finally said, his voice serious. "About the air sprite—"

I waved him off. "All in the past," I said.

"No, no. I need to say this." His brow furrowed as we continued walking, fast approaching the castle. "Clementine's brother left it with Oliver Andrel, the Andrel boy I hired in the bakery," he spoke, recounting the details. "Quite the exhausting little creature," he said. "Anyway, Oliver needed a day off. I offered to watch the sprite and promptly lost her, only later to find the devious thing tearing up your store."

I let out a breathy laugh. "I think the sprite had been hiding in your pocket the entire time." I turned to him, just briefly. "Or maybe she was just waiting to destroy my store. It all did seem very intentional." I smiled at him, and he met my grin with his own. "It is just like Bastian to own a sprite," I said. "Clem's family has been traveling for a while now. I'm not sure why Oliver agreed to keep it to begin with."

"He's a kind kid," Cyris answered. "Regardless." He stopped, turning to face me, and I turned to face him too, looking up into warm brown eyes. "I should have apologized sooner, Isla. I didn't even have the decency to help you clean up the mess." I saw something like regret flash across his features. "I was far too preoccupied with getting rid of the thing."

I tilted my head to the side, trying to convey what I felt. It really was fine. "It's okay, Cyris."

Slowly, too slowly, Cyris reached up, somewhat unsure of himself. He carefully trailed his thumb over my jaw, watching his finger as he moved it across my skin. I leaned into the touch, relishing in the feeling. "I'm glad it worked out the way it has, though," he confessed, his voice low.

The air seemed thick between us—like you could reach out and grab whatever feelings were mixing in the space.

All too soon, Cyris's hand dropped away. "Well," he said. "We had better head in."

I looked over, noting how close we were to the palace gates, and turned to make my way there.

When we stopped in front of the guard, he held out a long scroll, listing the names of those attending the ball. He nodded when he found we were on the list, and just before he moved to lead us into the palace, my eyes glanced left toward the other guard standing in the darkness—a face far too familiar for my liking.

I blinked and noted the way Cyris followed my gaze, no doubt seeing what I saw.

The guard didn't acknowledge me though, merely kept his eyes fixed forward as the former guard encouraged us to follow him in.

"Why is he here?" I whispered to Cyris as we trailed behind the guard through the palace halls on our way to the courtyard. I hardly had time to take in the ornately decorated walls on either side of us.

"He *is* a guard, at least," Cyris whispered. "That's enough explanation. Honestly, it should give us some reassurance, knowing he hadn't lied about working for the queen."

I nodded, but something about the knot forming in my belly kept me from being settled at his words. I wasn't sure of the guard's name or what he needed the Eliri for, but Cyris was right. He *did* work for the queen. Any other questions I had were pointless.

When we exited the castle and made our way into the courtyard, the entire garden glowed in the night, small lights filled with flame strung above the party. Tables and chairs lined the law, and all of Fairvein seemed to be in attendance. My eyes flicked across the way, catching sight of Sylvia smiling and laughing with the younger of the Andrel boys. She must have left rather quickly.

"Oliver's brother," Cyris said, tilting his head toward the two.

"So, it appears." I couldn't help the smile working at my lips. It wasn't like Sylvia to appear so happy. The boy certainly had to be a charmer.

Cyris moved in front of me, blocking my view. "Would you dance with me, Isla?" he said, holding his hand out.

The vibrant song floated through the air, drawing my attention to the large dance floor at the center of the party. I watched as couples twirled around, laughing and celebrating the start of the tourist season, or, more appropriately, the queen's brochure.

I took Cyris's hand, allowing him to guide me to the dance floor, where we promptly lost ourselves in music and plum wine, twirling and laughing just like the others. It had been the most glorious and carefree moment, not a single thing out of place.

Cyris and I slowed as one song ended, making way for a new tune to rise into the night. He reached out, resting his hand on my cheek and stroking gently as I smiled up at him.

"Are you happy, my dear Furious?" he asked, the twinkling lights highlighting every perfectly sculpted inch of his face.

"More than you know," I whispered, listening to the new song surrounding us and the sounds of laughter and joy. "More than you could ever know."

Cyris's gaze flicked briefly to my lips, a question written plainly on his face. I answered by moving forward, meeting him until those lips touched my own.

We kissed there on the dance floor, surrounded by the town we loved, ready for the rest of the night ahead of us.

Thirteen

As the dancing settled, a group of servants brought out a stage, setting it up just beyond the dance floor. It wasn't until we saw the queen that we realized the reason.

She walked up gracefully, her full gown shining gold in the night as two guards trailed behind her, guards I hadn't seen before. For that, I was thankful.

The queen stood at the center of the stage, her pointed ears decorated with numerous piercings, long braids descending down her back. She clapped once, demanding attention with the simple gesture, causing all eyes to turn to the stunning elven woman standing onstage. Queen Rosaline Cranefield.

"Good evening," she spoke, and Cyris gripped my hand where we stood, weaving his fingers through mine and smiling down at me once. I squeezed his hand, hoping he saw it as an encouragement. No matter what happened—who won, I would be glad for it. "First of all, thank you all for coming. It has been the most amazing night, and I have certainly felt welcomed by every single one of you who call Fairvein your home." Quiet murmurs floated through the crowd but quickly ceased as she continued speaking. "As you know, I am here to announce the shop owners who will be featured in my yearly travel brochure. Something I find great joy in, clearly." Her dark eyes sparkled as she scanned the crowd, and we all chuckled. "Well," she said, grabbing a scroll from one of the guards flanking her. "Let's not waste time. I would like to invite each of the winners to stop by my table following this announcement. It would be–" She paused, waving a hand through the air. "Oh, forget it," she said, a smile gracing her full lips. "Come see me later because I'd like to meet you. Let's get on with it, shall we."

My eyes stayed fixed on the stage, Cyris's hand warm in mine as she began reading off categories, naming the winners, and pausing for cheers. Cyris leaned in, pressing a gentle kiss to my temple. He smelled like plums and cinnamon again, and I found that it had become my favorite scent.

"Good luck," he whispered.

"You too."

"And," the queen announced, "bakeries and cafes." She glanced away from the scroll, looking out into the crowd. "Fairvein had quite a few of those." We chuckled, and I could feel the anticipation work its way down my spine as I leaned ever so slightly forward. "Cyris Buford," she announced, "for his delicious pastries and life-changing jam."

"Life-changing?" I said, turning to smile in congratulations. Cyris's shoulders were tense, and I nudged him. "Don't worry," I said. "I am equal parts disappointed and exceptionally happy."

"You mean it?" he asked.

My smile dropped, my face turning deathly serious. "When have I ever lied about my emotions?"

He chuckled, pushing his glasses further up his nose. "Good point."

"We do have one more category, one added after my scout found his way into one very peculiar store. It wasn't exactly open, he informed me, but he could see enough of it." Her smile widened. "Clementine Hyllian, for her shop of the extraordinary and curious."

I beamed up at the queen, excited to tell Clem when she returned to Fairvein after whatever adventure she had gone on.

"And I'll count that as a win," I said to Cyris. "Clem *did* have me watching the store in her absence. It's practically all my doing."

"Is it now?" He raised a brow, brown eyes settling on my face.

"Oh, absolutely," I said.

⇛⇛⇝ ⇜⇚⇚

"It's lovely to meet you, Cyris," Queen Cranefield said as soon as we approached the table to introduce ourselves.

"This is Isla," he said, gesturing to me.

"Ah, yes," the queen said. "Isla's Teas and Treats. Quite the shop you run. I've heard so much about you."

My cheeks stained pink, my head bowing as I accepted her words. "I hope you've only heard good things," I said.

Her eyes flicked from me to Cyris, one brow raised as a servant appeared behind her carrying a golden tray with a glass of wine atop it. "Interesting things, to be certain."

Cyris chuckled, and the queen reached for me with one hand. I accepted it gratefully, curtsying as I moved in closer. "Now," she whispered, "I do believe your shop was at the top of the list, but my scout informed me that your scones tasted nearly identical to the ones at the bakery." I smiled, looking away briefly. "That, and my scout happens to enjoy food. I promise to make it up to you, though. I firmly believe in your little tea shop, Isla Alden."

"Thank you," I spoke softly, feeling the lump forming in my throat.

The queen grabbed the wine glass from her tray, swirling the cup in front of her face. I had been standing close enough to catch a whiff of the liquid, the scent pulling on my memories in a way that made me feel uneasy. I fought to place it as she slowly raised the glass to her lips, my brows furrowed in concentration.

"Isla?" Cyris asked.

"No," I whispered, the name ramming into me with the force of an entire griffin falling to the ground. "Don't drink that!" I yelled, slapping the glass away from the queen's face.

Cyris quickly grabbed my arm, pulling me backward as if I had gone quite insane.

Her expression shifted—shock, confusion, complete and utter surprise. "What is the meaning of this?" she asked, staring at the plum wine bleeding into the grass below. I stared at the spot, certain of what the glass contained.

"Eliri," I whispered, shaking my head slightly. "The herb. It's used in healing salves but is poisonous when ingested. I'd know the scent anywhere. Slightly floral with hints of mint."

The queen looked at me, sizing me up, no doubt. She looked back at the servant who had gone sheet white. "I promise, Your Highness, I merely brought the drink out to you from the kitchen."

"And what would you know about this Eliri plant?" she asked, her features severe.

I turned my arm over, revealing the raised welt detailing a sun and a moon—the healer's mark.

"I see," she said, her lips pressing into a thin line. The queen turned to the servant, her tone laced with the authority of one who routinely sat on a throne. "Who gave you that glass?" she asked.

The man shook ever so slightly as we waited for an answer, the laughter and music dying down as elves, nymphs, and mortals alike paused to watch the scene unfold.

"One of your guards, Your Highness."

"A guard?" Cyris questioned. "Isla, do you think–"

"Does she think what?" the queen interrupted.

"Um." The nerves made my hands shake, fear working its way into my blood, flowing to every part of me as I tried to relay what had happened with her guard in the days prior.

"And you gave him this Eliri plant?" she asked, and my stomach dropped.

I felt ashamed, my cheeks heating with embarrassment. It had been so, *so* stupid. The guard, whoever he was, hadn't brought any paperwork. I had trusted him based on his uniform alone. That excuse didn't seem like enough. "It's commonly used in salves," I said. "I don't usually sell the dried herb itself, but I figured since he was wearing a uniform–" I trailed off, unable to finish my sentence.

The queen nodded before turning to a guard standing behind her, whispering something in his ear.

"You two will need to stay here," she said. "As well as the rest of the guests until we find the guard you described. I will have one of the servants bring you up to a room."

Cyris nodded, and the queen's eyes flicked suspiciously between us. "Two separate rooms, I might add."

Bile was rising in my throat as Cyris, and I followed the servant. I could only hope that they would find the guard–figure out the truth of what would happen.

If they couldn't, I didn't know what my fate would be, but something in the silence of the palace walls had my stomach churning, tears pricking my eyes.

They might as well have been walking us to the dungeons.

Fourteen

The palace room was cold despite the springtime just outside the window. The servant who had led me here started the fire upon my arrival, but the large space hadn't warmed much. The late lighting of the fire and the lack of any others in the room with me made the chill almost unbearable.

I sat in my gown, my cloak tied around my neck, as I fiddled with the skirt of my dress.

I couldn't help the way my knees bounced anxiously–the way my mind couldn't stop replaying the scene over and over. I did the right thing, that much I knew, but worry was like a thief, it robbed its victim of all joy, and true to the analogy, my joy had disappeared, replaced by the incessant fear that I would somehow be blamed for the queen's poisoned cup.

The night wore on, and I was certain the sun was about to make its appearance on the horizon, lighting up Fairvein in delicious pink light. It wouldn't help me, now. I would still be stuck in this room, praying to anyone who listened that the guard who had betrayed his queen would be found.

What motives did the guard have, anyway? The queen of Edessa had been dearly loved, her husband as well. I simply couldn't think of a reason for one of her own to turn on her so quickly.

I stood up, pacing the room until I felt my nerves settle–if only slightly.

The door to the bed chamber clicked open, and I found myself standing abruptly to see Cyris walking in behind one of the royal guards. His hair looked hopelessly mussed, as if he had been tugging the strands all night long.

"They found him," he said, his voice low as he halted in front of me, the guard still waiting by the door. "They found the guard, and he confessed."

My body longed to feel relief, and maybe it did, if only slightly. I still had questions, though. "You're certain?" I asked.

"Certain," he answered, his crooked smile easing the worry in my chest. "The guard had been dabbling in dark magic," Cyris said, his face turning severe. "Without knowing much, it appears that a dead queen can be used for a number of nefarious purposes. Her blood, her *hair*."

I fought the bile rising slowly in my throat. "I–"

"I won't speak of it anymore," Cyris said, noting my uncomfortable expression.

"And we are free to go?" I asked.

"Well," he began, "the queen would like to see *you* in particular first, and then yes, we are free to go."

I blew out a breath, picturing the guard in my mind. "He will be put to death, won't he?"

"Oh, for certain."

I shook my head, tears welling at the corners of my eyes. The night had been far more eventful than I had ever imagined, swinging between the highest of highs and the lowest of lows. "It's all my fault," I whispered, playing the scene over again.

Cyris grabbed my face gently, forcing me to look into his warm brown eyes. "No, Isla," he chuckled, "it's not." He brushed the stray tear sliding down my cheek, kissing the spot gently. "You are a hero," he said. "You saved the queen of Edessa. Not many can claim to have done that."

I laughed then, but the sound was tight and airy–more like releasing the tension of the night's events instead of finding amusement in what Cyris was saying. "Yeah," I said. "I suppose I did."

Cyris smiled, his gaze exuding pride. "Look at you," he said. "A hero, even without the *something extra* you thought you were missing." He stepped back, taking me in. "You are by far the most stunning creature I've ever beheld and the most talented healer I've ever met."

I laughed then–truly, and Cyris reached out to grab my hand.

"Let's go," he said. "It's time to see the queen."

Epilogue

Cyris poked his head into the kitchen, a suspicious look on his face as he greeted Sylvia before turning his attention to me.

My eyes narrowed, certain that something was amiss. "What?" I said–my tone flat.

"I have a surprise for you," he answered, stepping into the kitchen fully.

Sylvia chuckled next to me, turning to start the kettle for the morning. I didn't know if she knew what the surprise was, but in the weeks since the ball, I found that she seemed far less irritated–probably something to do with the Andrel boy, but I wasn't one to make such judgments.

"Okay," I said, peeling off my apron and following Cyris into the tea shop.

We had begun courting in earnest, and the entire town kept tabs on our every move now that the news was out. It didn't stop me from shoving Cyris out of my apartment before the sun rose each morning, vehemently demanding we don't cause a scene, telling him that all of his honor was at risk and he should consider that enough motivation to move a bit faster.

He always laughed while leisurely exiting through the front door, planting an obvious kiss on my lips. I couldn't say I didn't enjoy it.

Walking out onto the cobblestone, I noticed something standing by the bakery, tied to a post.

"A goat?" I questioned, my shock written plainly on my face.

Cyris laughed—a deep chuckle that pulled from the pit of his belly. "I thought he would be a nice gift," he said. "Plus, I could use the milk."

I stared at him, mouth agape and wondering what on earth he had been thinking when he went out to purchase such a ridiculous animal. My lens had been fully colored after struggling with Myrtle for an entire morning. There was not a single alternate universe in which I would have ever, *ever* wanted a goat as a gift.

"Surprise," he said, knowing full well I wouldn't enjoy this at all. "Don't worry." Cyris sidled up beside me, pressing a kiss to my temple. "It was more a gift for myself. I know you hate animals."

"I do not!" I denied, feeling insulted.

I looked down the street, squinting to make out the two figures walking toward us, one tall and dressed in the uniform of the queen's guard, the other wearing an extravagant and somewhat outlandish dress, her brown skin shimmering in the pink light of the sun.

"Clementine?" I said, not daring to believe what I was seeing.

"Isla!" she said, bursting forward before wrapping me in a warm hug. "How are you?" she asked, placing her hands on my shoulders and reeling back to get a good look at my face.

My smile stretched from ear to ear, my chest warming at the sight of my very best friend. "I'm good, but forget me," I said. "Where in all of Edessa have you been?" My eyes flicked briefly to the guard. Something about the way he stood next to her, the way his eyes softened each time his gaze slid her way, told me almost all I needed to know.

"I have so much to tell you," she said, pulling the brown satchel tighter across her body. I recognized the bag immediately, a gift I had given her what felt like forever ago.

"As do I," I said, Cyris moving to stand beside me and lacing his fingers through my own. "And I should start with news about your shop."

"My shop?" she questioned. "Everything seemed normal when I stopped there earlier."

"Oh, surely," I said, picturing the way her expression would light up when she heard the news about her feature in the brochure.

After the events during the ball, the queen had requested our presence before our departure, and while I hadn't won a feature in her travel guide, I certainly won a mention in the paper. In my opinion, *hero* was a bit of a strong word to use, but it brought business just the same.

"Why don't you two come in for tea?" I asked, nodding my head toward the door.

Clementine accepted, dragging the guard along with her behind me, and something about that seemed oddly fitting.

"I'll be right behind you," Cyris called. "I have to try and get the goat out back behind the bakery. The pen is already ready."

"Good luck," I hollered, smiling as I watched him struggle to pull the creature along.

We entered the tea shop, Sylvia filling the case with scones upon our arrival.

"As I said," I began, pulling up an extra chair so we would all fit at the table near the window. "You've missed so much." Clem took her seat next to the guard, her skin a few shades darker, as if she had spent days outdoors; I supposed she might have. "Let's start with the most unbelievable part of the tale."

"Does it have to do with the mention of your name in the paper?" she asked.

"No." I chuckled, brushing a stray strand of hair away from my face. "It actually has to do with Cyris."

ACKNOWLEDGMENTS

This novella was honestly one of the most fun books I've written, and I have plenty of friends to thank for this.

First of all, thank you Wednesday for creating the world with me and for pressuring me to start writing this by texting me with a million questions at midnight about the story I was planning. You created a cover in about two minutes for your own book, and it spurred me on into the realm of unhinged obsession. I don't usually like working with other people, but you are alright. Also, thank you for spelling griffin seven different ways in your manuscript and making my job harder.

Thank you McKayla, Shelby, and Becca for reading this book before it was fully edited. I cannot thank you enough for not judging my grammatical errors.

Thank you Reanna for proofing last minute. I'm sorry to put you under pressure like that, but I appreciate it all the same. I will try to learn how to use commas appropriately. No promises.

I want to thank Becca again for letting me use your scone recipe since I don't know how to bake, making the cutest videos, reviewing, and just overall being a wonderful bookish friend.

Finally, thank you to my husband. Thank you for asking questions like *why are your love interests always tall?* and *why do you use so many curse words when you write?* This book is for you. Thank you for cheering me on when I realized I didn't have the magic I needed to keep teaching in the classroom, and for encouraging me to open my own tea shop by writing tons of books. I love you more than you know.

Clementine's Parlor of the Extraordinary and Curious

Anxious for more time in Fairvein? Wondering what Clementine was doing?

Please enjoy the first chapter of the companion novella titled *Clementine's Parlor of the Extraordinary and Curious* by Monroe A. Wildrose.

ONE

I cradled the teapot in the crook of my arm, the lid securely stored away in the deep pocket of my periwinkle dress so as not to accidentally break it. The green glaze on the top and bottom of the clay reminded me of my best friend, and the daisy inlay in the center was too cute to pass up. Had I been swindled by the traveling peddler who had come through yesterday? Perhaps. After all, I didn't even know what the teapot's magical property was. I had little time to research it, but I could tell it was enchanted with some sort of magic. Had it been worth the gold rune globe I had traded for it? Who knew?

I skipped to the door and passed the sign that read *Islas Teas and Treats*. I pulled my skirt behind me, the dress's train having been embroidered with deep purple flowers and leaves. The top half of my full figure was prominently on display as well. The gown was a little too ornate and ostentatious for everyday wear, but that had never stopped me before, even as I got several looks from the few teashop patrons as I entered.

"Isla?" I called out, and her messy pile of hair popped up from behind the counter. She smiled, her fair and freckled face scanning my appearance, her thoughts writing across her features as she had them.

"Hello, Clem." She pulled a bundle of lavender up with her and set it on the counter.

"I've brought you something." I brandished the teapot.

"You give me too many gifts." My friend rolled her eyes as I sat on a bar stool.

"Let's call this a trade of services." I set the pot on the counter and pushed up one of my puffed sleeves to reveal a burn on the dark brown skin of my arm.

"Goodness, what did you do?"

"Self-heating skillet. Useful but dangerous."

"Sounds just like you." She turned and rushed about, getting some things together. She set a teapot trimmed in yellow leaves in front of me as she scurried to help her other customers.

I pulled the lid out of my pocket and set it on the pot, fiddling with it. Isla didn't come back for ten minutes, and I smiled as I heard her get roped into a conversation with an Old Lady Wren about her enchanted garden greens that had taken root in her prized rutabaga bed.

"Here." She poured some of the tea into a matching teacup when she got back to me. The liquid was mossy green but smelled of fresh strawberries. She disappeared into her back room and appeared, once again, with a small silver tin.

"Spread this on the burn next couple of days. It'll promote healing."

I pocketed it, nodding my thanks as I took a long draw of the tea. I nearly hummed at its sweet and floral taste.

"What's the teapot do?" she asked.

"Can't tell you that; you'll have to find out for yourself."

"What use is a magic teapot if I don't know what it does?"

"You'll figure it out." I took out a silver coin and put it on the bar. She pushed it back to me.

"Don't insult me, please." She poured the rest of the tea into a tall ceramic mug with a fitted lid. "Do you want a pastry to go?"

"No, thank you, not today." I looked up at the ceiling so as not to meet her eyes.

"No? You always take a pastry. I have orange scones today."

I met her eyes, my guilt welling up within me. Her one raised eyebrow and knowing gaze already guessing my motives.

"You know what, yes, I will take one. It sounds delicious."

A lie was not a lie if it was tiny and in the service of someone's feelings.

Her eyes never left mine as she went to the case to remove a scone. She set it into a paper box and slid it down the bar.

"Enjoy that." A thinly veiled threat lay behind her words. A threat of no real danger, and I bit my bottom lip to keep from laughing.

"Oh, I will, surely. I'll enjoy this...at home..."

"Hmmm," she said, tucking a strand of stray hair back into her bun.

I laughed as I exited the shop with my mediocre scone and exceptional tea in my hands, heading directly across the street.

Cyris was a newcomer to Fairvein. His shop opened, and people had been hesitant to try it at first. The people of Fairvein were much more comfortable with the known than the new. However, he had won us all over... all except Isla, that is.

"Miss Hyllian!" His smooth voice came to me before I could even look up to find him.

Cyris was a handsome sort of man with a short, well-kept beard, pale skin, and wire-framed glasses. He was charming and friendly, which is part of why he had won our community so quickly.

"Hello, Cyris; please call me Clementine, for goodness sake."

"Well then, Clementine, I have your order all ready right here. He produced an ivory box tied with golden ribbon. I peered inside and smiled at the half-dozen brioche donuts filled with vanilla pastry cream and roasted strawberry jam– the outsides of them coated in pink strawberry sugar. It took everything in me not to tear open the box and devour one on the spot.

"They are so lovely, thank you." I slid him his payment as he smiled at my exuberance.

"Can I interest you in a cup of tea?" he asked, pointing to a large vessel of unappetizing tea and some unimpressive cups sitting on the counter.

I looked at the cup in my hand and then at him as a mischievous grin split his face.

"You may have a way with dough, Mr. Cyris, but I'd leave the tea-making to the shop across the way; if you value your life."

He greeted my words with a soft smile, and I could tell he would not leave well enough alone. To tussle with Isla was a dangerous game, but I didn't warn him. He would learn on his own.

I exited the shop and set my scone box on top of the other one. I tried to figure out the best way to get out of the door with my hands full and a dress intended for a ballroom. Its tulle layers were a handsome sight, though it made getting in and out of regular places quite the challenge.

"Have you no shame, Clemintine Hyllian?" Isla's voice came to me just as I managed to get the patisserie door closed. I froze and looked across the way.

"None at all, actually." I headed down the street back to my shop and heard her scoff after me.

Fairvein was a tourist island. The shops were quaint and cozy, and the light seemed softer and more welcoming. It was as if the suns themselves saw fit to bless us. And while we were very slow during the fall and winter months, the traffic in the late spring and summer more than made up for it. We were a destination for the wealthy, who loved to buy our food and wares and be seduced by the magic of our affectionate town. Fairvein itself was built around a castle where the royal family, The Cranefeilds, came to live in the summer. So naturally, we drew a high-born clientele.

My shop, Clemintine's Parlor of the Extraordinary and Curious, was a trove of magical, enchanted, and unusual items. Items I traded, collected, bought, and sold. The windowsills and counter spaces were absolutely packed with trinkets so that you could come in and see something new every time. It was a two-story building with an overrun garden in front and an iron half-fence that barely kept it contained. The plants just wild enough to look charming but not menacing. I didn't want to seem like a witch after all—just an eccentric human who dabbled in the magical.

I kicked open the door to my shop and walked inside, looking for a clear surface to set down my sweet treats.

"Miss Clementine Hyllian," A voice came to me, and I shrieked in fright as the box of pastries flew to the ground. I clutched the clay mug to my chest, spilling some of the green tea onto the front of my dress.

The sitting room in the middle of my shop held three velvet couches and a large glass table with gold legs. Sitting in one of those chairs was a royal elven guard.

His expression was severe, and his long black hair was tied behind him. He wore a sheer mask over his nose and mouth, the soft cream color of his skin contrasting with the black fabric. His heavy-lidded eyes peered out at me as if he were startled by my cry. *He had scared me; what was he so shocked about?*

"Are you Clementine Hyllian?" No apology, no remorse, and his face, or what I could see, had gone even more staunch than before.

"Indeed, I am." I reached down to pick up my donuts which had now been badly jostled.

"I am Enver of the queen's elven guard, and I am looking for a magical item."

<u>CYRIS'S SCONE RECIPE</u>

2 cups of flour

1/4 cup of sugar

4 tsp baking powder

1/2 cup butter

1/2 tsp salt of salt

1/4 tsp cream of tartar

1 egg

2/3 cup of cream

- Preheat oven to 350 degrees

- Cut butter into dry ingredients

- Mix wet ingredients

- Knead together any additional ingredients you would like to add

- Make into a ball and flatten. Cut into a triangle or rectangle, and then cut into approximately 16 triangles

- Place on baking sheet lined with parchment paper

- Coat with milk/cream and sprinkle coarse sugar on top

- Bake for 20-25 minutes

- Enjoy

<u>Isla's Scone Recipe</u>

See Cyris's scone recipe, but forget the cream, add a little bit of water instead, and maybe overcook them.

You can also undercook them. Whatever you like to make them taste like the dust from an old attic.

About Author

Emma Steinbrecher typically writes New Adult Fantasy as well as New Adult Romantic Comedy under the pen name Emmie J. Holland.

She lives in Ohio with her two dogs, her son, and her husband.

When she's not writing, she enjoys hiking, learning new hobbies, and reading.

If you're anxious to read any of her other works, here is a list of the books.

A Clan of Wolves Duology

A Clan of Wolves by Emma Steinbrecher (Book 1)

A House of Witches by Emma Steinbrecher (Book 2)

The Death Hunting Trilogy

The Death Hunting by Emma Steinbrecher (Book 1)

The Raidan Awakening by Emma Steinbrecher (Book 2)

The Light Conquering by Emma Steinbrecher (Book 3)

Emmie J. Holland

Te Unbelievable Misadventures of Olive Finch by Emmie J. Holland

Pride, Pancakes, & Paris by Emmie J. Holland